Jack Rubin is a police officer. He is dismissed after five years, accused of accepting bribes. He sets up in business as a private investigator and soon finds that his main occupation is to collect bad debts and harass vulnerable losers. However, his luck seems to turn when he takes on Mohammed Ali Malik, a Pakistani, as his partner.

Rubin, an atheist from a Jewish family, is a totally amoral tough guy and womaniser, and Malik, a Muslim and family man, loyal, frightened of his own shadow, are chalk and cheese. Yet, in spite of deep differences, their partnership seems to succeed. They have agreed one rule: never to discuss religion - and always to make their own tea and coffee.

DEEP BLOOD

DEEP BLOOD

Jack Rubin

DEEP BLOOD

EMMA
STERN
PUBLISHING

An Emma Stern Publication

Copyright © Jack Rubin 2016

The right of **Jack Rubin** to be identified as author of this work
has been asserted in accordance with sections 77 and 78 of the
Copyright, Designs and Patents Act 1988.

A CIP catalogue record for this title is available from the British Library.

ISBN: 978-1-911224-06-8

Published in 2016

Emma Stern Publishing
107 Fleet Street
London
EC4A 2AB

www.emmastern.com
www.facebook.com/emmasternpublishing
Email: editorial@emmastern.com
Email: marketing@emmastern.com

Printed in Great Britain

Chapter One

The door was thrown open noisily.

I thought the glass was going to shatter.

We expected a large man to stride in. The white guy who entered the office was, in fact, little. Looked as if he couldn't knock the skin off a rice pudding.

'You Rubin?' the man asked belligerently.

Little men are often belligerent. As if they have something to prove, which is often the case.

'I am Mr Rubin,' I said quietly. 'Jack Rubin. My name's on the door.'

From where I sat I could see the glass door with the company name embossed in black. **Jack Rubin Associates.**

'And this' – I gestured to my business partner – 'is Mr Malik.'

We exchanged handshakes. Briefly. No warmth.

'My name is Burnside,' the short guy said.

'Won't you sit down, Mr Burnside?'

He sat down but he was clearly agitated.

'Tea or coffee?' I said.

'Neither,' he snapped. 'I want to get down to business.'

'Me too, Mr Burnside,' I said. 'But I think better with a dose of caffeine in my hand.'

Malik switched on the Morphy Richards. He knows the routine. I made the coffee, black. I looked round the office. It looked shabby. After Burnside had gone, I'd get Malik to start cleaning up.

'Now, Mr Burnside,' I said, sitting down again, cradling my mug. 'If you'd like to tell me how we can assist you.'

I choose my words carefully in situations like these. Never ask a client what's troubling them. Never say or do anything to upset them. After all, a client means money, and I don't exactly have a treasure house of clients. On the other hand, I never lick their arses either. Hence my insistence on making coffee first.

He stared out of the window and across the Square to the railway station.

I glanced across at Malik. He shrugged his shoulders. Not enough for Burnside to notice but enough for me to see.

'My wife.....I.....Mr Rubin, I need help.'

I noted that Burnside's lips were thin and almost bloodless.

'Your wife,' I said softly.

He'd get round to his story eventually.

'I need your help to find my wife,' Burnside said.

No problem. If he paid me enough, I'd search for his bloody cat or his missing dog.

'Carry on, Mr Burnside.'

He was wearing a lightweight suit, green, just right for the hot weather we were having. It gets damned hot this time of year. His shirt had blue stripes. The blue and green did not match. Perhaps his wife usually chose his clothing of a morning, and she, on his own admission, was not there right now.

I sipped my hot coffee. Give him time. He'd get round to it. When he'd stopped fidgeting and biting his finger nails. He was certainly restless. Could not stay still for as much as a second. Something was troubling this guy. Maybe he loved her very much. Or perhaps he'd been playing around and she had walked out, declaring that enough was enough.

You....you're not too busy are you, Rubin...er, Mr Rubin?'

'We are in fact very busy,' I said.

My first lie of the day. While Malik and I were not exactly on our uppers, we certainly needed money to come into the business account. My last two jobs had taken much of my time and I hadn't earned a penny. Malik had berated me for that. I told him to mind his own business, but I only said that because I knew he was right.

'Tell me about your wife, Mr Burnside,' I said.

'Jessica,' he said at last. 'Jessica. Jessica Connolly.'

'That's her maiden name,' I said softly.

'What?'

For a little guy, Burnside had a big voice.

'Isn't your wife Jessica Burnside?'

He sighed.

'I suppose you'll have to know,' he said. 'She's not my wife.'

'No problem,' I said, and I smiled.

When you want someone for a paying client, it is as well to smile, so long as the situation is appropriate. Someone comes in the office and tells me they have killed their mother, I don't smile. Not that anyone has yet come to see me and confessed to murder.

'She's missing,' he said mournfully.

'What exactly do you mean by......by missing? Has she run away. Has she gone somewhere without telling you where. Or has she, perhaps, been abducted?'

Burnside's tongue flicked across his thin lips.

'Aren't you going to make notes?' he asked.

'When you begin to give us details,' I said.

'I'd rather talk to you alone,' Burnside said.

'Mr Malik is my trusted associate,' I said.

.No problem,' Malik said, speaking for the first time since Burnside had burst into the office.

Malik got to his feet and made for the door. He knows the routine. If there's money involved, he'll accept an insult.

'I'll pop downstairs and get some scones,' Malik said.

OK, Mr Burnside,' I said. 'Jessica isn't your wife. Is she your partner?'

He shook his head.

'Girl friend?'

Again he shook his head.

Now it was my turn to sigh, but I suppressed it.

'Hey, man!' I said, 'if I'm to help you, you need to give me something to go on.'

I could see that he wanted to talk but at the same time he was reluctant. I needed to be patient. I wanted this guy's money. My bank manager wanted his money too.

'Great danger,' Burnside said at last. 'Jessica's in great danger.'

'What makes you think that, Mr Burnside?'

'I'm not stupid!' he flared angrily.

'I never suggested you were,' I said quietly.

When dealing with a man who is nervous, agitated, and seems to want to pick an argument, there are several roads to go. You can smack him in the jaw and walk away. But if he is a potential client, a possible source of cash, it pays to be patient. I know what it is to be patient. I used to be a cop. Five years in total, until I was kicked off the force, accused of something I did not do. In those five years, I learned to be quiet and observant, when the task demanded it. Names may have changed in the world of crime prevention and detection, but much remains the same. Plus ça change, and all that. You can replace governments, laws, institutions, and the people who run them, but you can't fundamentally alter human nature.

Now I'm a private investigator, but the same rules apply. It isn't like what you see in the movies or on TV shows; there's no simple linear progression from crime committed to crime punished, and we all go home at the end of each episode with a joke and a laugh. And at this moment I was being quiet and observant. I noted that Burnside's hair had been dyed brown. I was sure he wasn't wearing a rug on his head. Some people, men and women, like to hide grey hair.

'Start at the beginning, Mr Burnside,' I said gently.

'I.....I'm doing this for a friend,' he said.

How many times have I heard that one?

'So what is the name of your friend, Mr Burnside?'

'You come highly recommended,' Burnside said, avoiding my question.

'Oh yes!. And who is my secret benefactor? Abel Magwitch?'

Burnside looked bewildered, did not pick up the literary reference.

'Superintendent Silcock,' he said.

'A good man,' I said. 'An honest copper.' Silcock and I go back some time, and if he was good enough to recommend me, I was happy to return the favour. 'And now, what is the name of your friend?'

'I can't tell you that,' Burnside replied.

Truth to tell, I was beginning to be pissed off by Burnside.

'My friend is willing to pay well for your trouble, Mr Rubin.'

'To find out where Jessica is.'

He nodded.

I almost smiled. This seemed to be nothing more serious than a domestic upset. Until Burnside added,

'We think her life is in danger,' Burnside said.

'And what evidence have you for that?'

'I think he wants to kill her,' Burnside said.

'Who? Your friend?'

'No! Someone who knew Jessica in the old days.'

The old days. How often do I hear that? What's wrong with living in the present?

'Someone without a name, no doubt,' I said.

Burnside did not pick up on the irony.

'Frank,' Burnside said. 'Frank Conteh.'

'An Italian?' I said, thinking he meant Conti.

'A black man?' he said.

'An African?'

Yes. Do you know him?' Burnside asked.

I shook my head.

'No. Have you met him, Mr Burnside?'

'I'm a respectable businessman,' Burnside snorted. 'I don't mix with criminal scum.'

'Tell me, Mr Burnside. Do you have a photo of Jessica?

He searched in his jacket and produced a snap. It was one taken in a booth, and they are not always of good quality. But quality or not, I could see immediately that Jessica

Connolly was a looker. A real nice piece of feminine pulchritude. It would be a pleasure finding her, I told myself.

A real pleasure. And having found her.......

Chapter Two

'Four grand?' Malik kept on saying. 'Four grand?' and skipping round the room on his tiny feet.

'Plus disbursements,' I said.

'But what if his cheque bounces?' Malik asked.

'Then we strop looking for Miss Connolly,' I said.

'Can I look at her photo again?' Malik asked.

'A real corker,' I said. 'How I'd like to get between her thighs.

Malik salivated over the photograph of Jessica Connolly.

'Time to celebrate,' I said.

'Let's go for a good meal,' Malik said.

I shook my head.

'You get those at home every day, Malik. Be brave. Go for some other place. One that doesn't have rats and cigarette butts on the kitchen floor,'

'Like what?'

I wasn't sure, so we settled for a place out of town. I had meat, veg, the whole works. Malik ordered an assortment of vegetables. I still cannot get him to give up on halal.

'She enjoys dancing?' I said.

'What?'

Malik's mouth was stuffed with courgette.

'Jessica. She likes to dance. Burnside said she could dance the night through and still want more.'

I smiled contently.

'Finding Jessica Connolly is going to be a pleasure, and when I do.......'

'You've only seen her face,' Malik said. 'The rest of her, she may be fat and bow-legged.'

'So long as she has a pulse,' I said.

'What is going to be your first move, Mr Rubin?'

Malik is always formal. He never calls me Jack or Rubin. Always the mister.

'Burnside said that if we find Conteh, he'll lead us to Jessica.'

'And you believe him?'

'Should I have doubted him?' I asked.

'He was furtive,' Malik said.

'Agitated,' I said.

'You can tell a liar by his face,' Malik added.

'No you can't,' I said. 'There's no art to finds the mind's construction in the face.'

'Shakespeare again?'

'We'll make a scholar of you yet, Mr Malik.

'Four thousand grand,' he said happily.

'Yes, and if you could drink alcohol, I'd order a bottle of good wine.'

'Well, as this is a special occasion -'

'No, I wouldn't want to be the cause of you flouting your religious laws, daft as they are.'

Malik rubbed his nose vigorously, a sure sign that he was in some sort of turmoil.

As we ate, I confided in my associate that Burnside had left an address and a telephone number before leaving the office. I had told him that if he heard from Frank he should contact me immediately. Preferably by phone.

To all this, Burnside agreed. And he had written the cheque without hesitation, which suggested he had enough funds to cover it, or he knew damn well it was made of rubber.

I had escorted Burnside along the corridor and down the steps to the street level, where I spotted Malik skulking in the doorway of the café, waiting for Burnside to leave.

Yes, Burnside was almost certainly a liar, or at least keeping information from me, information that might well be relevant to finding Jessica.

As soon as Burnside disappeared along John Green Street, I whistled to attract Malik's attention.

There is talk of doing away with cheques and I for one shall not weep.

I'd already decided that I was not going to wait the three or four days for the cheque to clear. I was anxious to discover if Jessica Connolly - Burnside's Jessica - was as gorgeous in real life as she appeared to be from her photograph.

So Jessica loved to dance. Very well, although I'm not a good dancer myself, I decided that I'd be spending a few evenings in clubs and dance halls.

'That was a good luncheon, Malik,' I said, once we were back in the office.

'You are the only person I know who says luncheon and not lunch,' he replied.

'So?'

'It's a bit....you know....weird.'

I smiled in response. Let him have his bit of fun. After all, we were several grand better off than when we'd first met.

'In fact,' he said, 'in many ways you are a very weird person, Mr Rubin.'

'It takes one to know one,' I said. And added: 'Four grand. How weird is that?'

'Plus disbursements,' Malik said.

We both laughed out loud.

Chapter Three

That same evening I went to a disco in town.

This is not my kind of scene. For one thing I don't like the music that is played. And I don't need to suffer noise and sweat in order to pull a woman. I value quietude and the opportunity to be away from people. If you said that I'm antisocial, you wouldn't be far wrong.

Burnside had told me Jessica liked dancing, and could dance the night away, so it made sense to go to a place where people dance. It was not the line of duty that made me go down to the Disco, but the prospect of earning my four thousand big ones. Burnside had valued Jessica at four grand - plus disbursements - so she must be much more than just a good-looking babe.

I ordered a soft drink and found a table to sit at. A tabled in a corner, with a strong wall behind me. There were four chairs but I was alone. Even at thirty plus, I realised I was older by more than a decade than most of the people there, whether they were drinking, eating - food was available - or dancing.

I wanted to look around. Later, perhaps, I might show Jessica's photograph to the doormen and bouncers, or even the bar staff.

A man joined me at my table. No so much as a by your leave, or are these chairs taken.

'So, how's life, Jack?' he said.

I looked at him. His face was familiar but I couldn't quite place him.

He smiled at me in a cheeky and cheerful way.

'Long time, no see, Jack,' he said, clearly enjoying the advantage he had over me.

When he smiled, he showed blackened teeth. I prefer my drinking companions to have some measure of personal dental hygiene.

'Ken Gee,' I said at last, dragging his name from the filing cabinet that is our memory.

He smiled again, pleased that I had remembered him.

'When did you get out, Ken?'

Now the little ferret was smiling no longer.

'I served two years,' he said, 'two stinking years, and you put me there, Jack, my friend.'

'Wrong, Ken,' I said. 'Wrong on two counts.'

'Eh?'

He had clearly not learned manners while serving time for nicking motor cars big time. Grand Theft Auto, as the Americans call it.

'First,' I said sternly. 'I did not put you away. That was the judge. Second, you little shit, I am not your friend. If you must talk to me, you call me Mr Rubin. Got that? OK?'

I kept my voice low but Ken Gee, thick and stupid as he is, was clearly in no doubt of what I was saying to him.

He took out a packet of tobacco and some Rizla paper and started to roll a cigarette with one hand. A trick he'd no doubt learned while he was doing his porridge.

'Why'd you spend time rolling when you could buy a pack of cigarettes?'

'Cancer, mate....er, Mr Rubin.'

There is a belief that roll-ups are safer in that regard. The research evidence points toward the danger remaining whatever you smoke. I detest the taste and smell of cigs, mainly, perhaps, because I too was once addicted to nicotine.

'What's wrong with calling you Jack? That's your name, innit?'

'My first name is for my friends,' I said, aware, even as I said it, that I have no friends.

The streets, bars and discos always attract the likes of Kenneth Gee, on the look out for a fast buck that doesn't require too much expenditure of energy. In other words, lazy swine. Who'd rather make big money nicking motor cars to order, and selling them on, than trying an honest day's work.

'I'm straight now, Mr Rubin. I've learned my lesson,' he said.

That's what they all say.

'Are you employed?'

He was not wearing a suit. Just a pair of stone-washed jeans and a tee-shirt. The shirt was much too large for him. It covered his belt as well as his torso. I knew the reason why. If I'd been on the door I'd have told him to get lost and come back in something more suitable, but it seemed to be a slack night, and Ken obviously had the entrance price.

'I get by,' he said.

Which meant he was drawing benefits and as likely as not doing jobs on the side, such as climbing on church roofs to nick lead, or cutting through cables to extract the copper. With a bit of luck the soft sod would saw through a live wire and electrocute himself.

'That isn't what I asked you, Gee. I asked if you were employed.'

'You lousy cops! You're all the same. Asking questions. Never letting a man forget -'

'Cut the crap, Ken,' I said harshly.

There was no point telling him I was no longer a copper.

He was surprised when I changed tack and offered to buy him a drink. I had my reasons. One was that a weasel like Ken Gee could keep his ears open. Any sighting of Jessica Connolly and he could report back to me.

'I'll tell you what, Ken. You keep quiet about my being a copper and I won't mention you're carrying a knife.'

His hand went immediately to his waist belt. I also noted that he was left-handed. That kind of knowledge can be useful when dealing with little shits like Ken.

'I gotta go out for a smoke,' he said.

But before he had a chance to move, there was a flurry of activity at the main entrance. A big man walked in. He was tall and he looked hard. He was wearing a two-piece suit, baggy, and in need of an iron. If there was going to be a fight in the place this evening I'd want to be on the same team as the big man. He had about him a look of danger, as if when he was around anything could happen. His hair was cut short, in a version of a Mohican. The kind that some black men choose. Yes, the newcomer was as black as it is possible for a black man to be.

I watched the man walk to the bar. People moved to make room for him. He ordered a Coke.

Ken Gee's eyes were bright with admiration. A big guy, with muscled shoulders, who could walk to a bar and order a soft drink. Ken would have liked to be that cool.

'Do you know him, Ken?'

'Who doesn't?'

'I don't,' I said.

'He's been away.'

'Inside?' I said.

'No. From what I heard, he was getting away from the heat.'

Ken Gee liked to think of himself as a man who understood the talk of the street.

I took out a twenty note.

'Mine's a still orange.'

Ken was happy for the chance to go to the bar. He grabbed my note and scurried off, his need for nicotine temporarily forgotten. The tough black man, muscled, mean, was the kind of guy he wanted to be. The kind, no doubt, that he tried to get close to while inside the big house. That Ken Gee took it up the arse, I did not doubt.

The black man had turned. He wanted to survey the whole area, and keep his back to the bar, for safety's sake. It always pays to know where danger may come from. I'd have done the same.

Ken went straight to the part of the bar where the man was standing. He smiled at the man, a stained and unattractive smile. The man nodded politely but did not speak.

Ken came back to the table, carrying my orange and a beer for himself. Beer in a plastic container. Glass in a place like this can lead to people being cut.

'OK, Ken,' I said, sipping orange. 'Who is this man?'

'You mean! You don't know?'

'Would I be asking you if I knew?' I said to the little twerp.

'That's Frank,' Ken Gee said, excitement in his eyes. 'The man himself. Frank Conteh.'

Chapter Four

Being a detective, either with the force or as a private investigator, is nothing like you might imagine from the movies and TV. It isn't all fast cars, punch ups and bedding glamorous girls - though in the third department, I try not to lose any opportunities. I have no particular preferences. In the dark, or with a paper bag over the head, they are all pretty much the same.

But the point I am making is that it isn't all excitements. There are hours and hours of just watching and waiting, of following someone, or waiting for them to emerge from a house. It's at times like these that I, for one, am pleased that motor cars have radios. The kind of music I like is always drives away boredom, and is usually a solace that no other art form ever compares with.

Let's take this evening. Normally I wouldn't choose to sit as daft as a brush in a disco allowing shit to pour into my ears. I had chosen it because of Jessica. She liked dancing, Burnside said. Then who should walk ion to the bar than

Frank Conteh? I'll not insult you with talk of predestination and chance, and al;l that balls.

I kept my eyes on Frank Conteh, still standing at the bar taking his soft drink. I decided that when Frank left, I would follow him. Find Frank Conteh and you'll find Jessica. That's what Burnside had said and he couldn't be a complete and utter liar. Could he?

'I need a ciggie,' Ken said. 'OK, Mr Rubin?'

I nodded my assent. As far as I was concerned his usefulness was at an end.

He stood up and walked swiftly to the door, a slave to nicotine.

Frank remained alone. No one approached him. No women or girls seeking to touch him for a drink or for sex.

He checked his wrist watch. An old-fashioned man, our Frank. These days, fewer people than ever wear wrist watches; they prefer to rely on cell phones and that kind of thing.

Then, to my surprise he walked across the dance floor to the far side of the room. It was now that I noticed, for the first time, a door in the corner marked *Private*. He did not knock and the door wasn't locked. Frank turned the handle and went inside.

What happened next was the real surprise. A man entered the disco. He stood at the door briefly, framed by it.

He looked round, taking in the scene. Then he strode purposefully across the room, which was large, and went unerringly to the far corner and the door marked *Private*. He tried the door and discovered that it was unlocked. He went inside. The guy was Mr Burnside, who'd set this investigation up in the first place.

At that moment, the wretched Ken Gee came back, stinking to high heaven of cigarette smoke and stale sweat, the rotten little weasel. He sat down with evident satisfaction.

I kept my eyes on the far door. Neither Frank nor Burnside came out.

'Ready for another drink, Mr Rubin?'

This was his way of trying to bum me for another drink.

'Who owns this place, Ken? Do you know?'

'No idea,' he said.

I took out my cell phone and chose Malik's number.

Malik answered immediately. I asked him to hang on. I turned to Ken Gee.

'This is a private call, Ken,' I said.

He shrugged his shoulders - or what passed for shoulders in his weak body.

'I'm not listening,' he said.

'Too true you're not,' I said. 'Find somewhere else to sit, or something else to do.'

'Somethin' else? Like what?'

'Go out in the street and case the cars,' I said.

'Case the cars?' he repeated like a parrot.

'It's what you do, isn't it? Nicking motors.'

'Here -'

'It's what you served two years for. Grand Theft Auto.'

'That's not fair, Mr Rubin.'

'No, it isn't. Now leave me alone,' I said.

'You lousy coppers. You're all the same.'

He scowled, stood up, and slouched over to the bar.

I opened my mobile telephone, told Malik where I was.

'Who was that?' Malik asked.

'Never mind him. He's a thief, a liar and a loser.'

'Shall I come down and join you?' Malik asked.

'Stay where you are. Tell me who owns this place,' I said. 'Do you know?'

Let me see.'

Now it was Malik's turn to keep me waiting. I could almost hear the wheels of his brain turning.

'It used to be a Greek,' Malik said at last. 'A Turkish Cypriot.'

'Balaban?'

'Yes, but he sold it to.....let me think.....Suleiman,' he said with a shout of glee that must have surprised Mona, his wife. 'Suleiman Chopdat.'

The name meant nothing to me.

'Yes, Suleiman Chopdat. Choppie.'

'Do you know him, Malik? Do you attend the same mosque?' I said.

'He's not from Pakistan,' Malik said. 'Somewhere in the Middle East. Iran, maybe.'

Malik talked and I listened but kept my eyes glued to the door.

When finally I ended the call, we had been talking for about thirty minutes. Malik is only really alive when he is talking. Thirty minutes and more and neither Frank nor Mr Burnside had emerged.

I walked outside. Perhaps there was a back entrance. I'd have been surprised if there had not.

I was just in time to see a Merc pulling out of the back yard. I could make out a driver but tinted windows made it difficult to be sure of the occupants of the car. I could make out three figures. They appeared to be male figures.

No prizes, Rubin, I told myself, for guessing who the three men were.

Chapter Five

'Surely,' I said, 'one or two must have made moves on you.'

'More than one or two,' Brigid laughed.

'But you're not that kinda girl,' I said.

Sergeant Brigid Riley of the Metro force. We were out together, enjoying a meal at Paul's Place, one of the best and the dearest restaurants in the town.

'It isn't simply that women don't turn me on,' Brigid said. 'It's the moustaches.'

'I don't mind lezzies having moustaches,' I said. 'But do they have to wax 'em?'

Brigid smiled.

'We're being very politically incorrect, Jack,' she said.

'You don't follow that shit, Bridge, do you?'

'These days, you've no choice. Things have changed, even from your day. How long has it been?'

'Five years,' I said. 'Five years, but I don't feel that I've fully escaped yet.

Brigid cut meat from her leg of lamb, delicately, using her knife and fork. I'd have used my fingers - quicker, easier. I had soon cleared my plate of the sausages and mashed potato. Bangers and mash in a tower, with thick brown gravy on top, and with prices higher than the topless towers of Ilium.

Brigid wiped her lips.

'Hm, yeah! The food here is good,' she said.

Then she fixed me with her eyes, as she doubtless did every day at work when dealing with suspects and villains.

'What are you after, Jack?'

'After?'

'Come off it,' she said. 'Five years and I hear nothing, except at second hand. Now, out of the blue -'

'You think I'm after something.'

'I'm sure you are.'

'OK,' I said. 'It's a fair cop. I am after your body.'

'Oh, I know that, 'she said, smiling. 'You can't see a woman without wanting to get her into bed. Or the back of your car.'

'I never had you in my bed or the back of a car,' I said, pretending to protest.

'No,' Brigid replied. 'It was in the locker room, after a game of squash.'

'You shouldn't have come into the men's changing rooms, should you?'

She shook her head and smiled again.

'You came into the ladies section, Mr Rubin.'

'That was a risky thing to do,' I said.

I remembered. She was undressed, apart from a pair of white knickers and black knee length boots. She had placed her right foot on the chair, to make it easier for me. But I had not found it easy, for young Brigid Riley was still a virgin.

'It was a rushed business, as I remember,' I said. 'I'd like to make it up to you.'

The waitress came to take the plates away and give us the dessert menu.

'I can't resist puddings,' I said.

I chose apple crumble and custard. Brigid asked for treacle pudding with cream.

'So, Jack, apart from the sex,' she said, 'what's the real reason you asked me out?'

I told her my reason, in part, at least, and her eyes opened wide again.

'It's more than my job's worth, Jack,' she said, 'you must know that.'

'It's not like the old days,' I said, 'when you'd have to smuggle files out on the office and back in the next day. Now, with computers -'

'Yes, but.....'

'Just running a check on three people. That isn't asking too much,' I said.

Our puddings arrived at the table.

'Apple crumble,' I said.

The young waitress, a young girl, probably a student earning pin money, blushed deeply.

'Are you a student?' I asked.

She nodded.

'Wits.'

'I wish you well,' I said.

As the girl walked away from our table, Brigid smiled broadly.

'Jack Rubin. Always was a charmer.'

'A bit young, though,' Brigid said, sounding every inch the police sergeant.

'If she's over the age of consent,' I said, 'it isn't illegal.'

We ate our puddings. Afterwards, we ordered coffee and moved to the lounge upstairs, where there are deep sofas.

'So, Bridge,' I said as soon as we were seated comfortably with hot coffee in our hands. 'Can you help me?'

'It's asking a lot, Jack.'

'Yes, but not too much.'

'Much too much,' she said.

I refrained from looking disappointed. But I needed her to assist me. I had to find as much as I possibly could on Burnside, Suleiman Chopdat and Frank Conteh.' There had to be something in police files on at least two of them. About Burnside, I was unsure. All I knew was, that he is a liar and that is not yet an offence.

'And what if I'm sussed out and lose my job,' Brigid said, rubbing the froth of the coffee from her upper lips.

'In that event, I'll employ you,' I said, without hesitation.

'No, seriously, Jack.'

'I am being serious,' I said.

'Would you really?'

'Yes. But make sure you don't get caught. You have as good career ahead of you in the force. You've dome well to reach sergeant already. Next step, Inspector. But another thing: I cannot afford to set you up with early retirement and a good pension.'

Brigid smiled thinly. It was the outward sign of her concern. She wanted to help me, for old time's sake. But she also knew that she would be breaking the rules, passing sensitive information to an outside person, a third party.

'Don't bring documents out. Scan them and send them to me electronically,' I said.

'Do you think they can't check?' she asked.

'Use another office, and don't use any names. No names, no pack drill,' I said.

She sighed. 'If only it was that easy.'

'Were,' I said.

'What?'

'Sorry, Bridge, it's just me being pedantic.'

We finished our coffees and I ate the After Eights intended for both of us. I was always something of a chocoholic.

I paid with the company debit card. The cost of the two meals and the accompanying drinks was high, but Burnside was paying. Or would be, if his cheque cleared.

Outside, the evening was warm.

'Back to my place?' I said, putting my arm round her should in what I hoped was both protective and seductive.

'You still living on a mountain top?' Brigid asked.

'I'll drive fast,' I said.

'Don't exceed the speed limits, will you?'

'Would I dream of it, with an officer of the law sitting beside me?'

Within thirty minutes we had showered together and were in bed. She was not a virgin. I had been the first to see to that, and no doubt others had followed me.

She was not a natural blond. I never expected she would be.

And before we fell asleep, she assured me that she would find as much information as possible on the the names I had given her.

I silently congratulated myself. I have not lost my touch. I had wanted to have sex with her and spend the night in the same bed. It wasn't just a case of my being a conniving swine, though I can be that too, if occasion demands.

Chapter Six

Getting into a maximum security prison is never easy. Not unless you have committed murder, and then the problem is getting out again.

HMP Wakeford is a high-security prison for men typically in security categories A and B. It was originally constructed late in the 16th century, right on this spot. Then, it was known as a House of Correction. It still is, in many ways.

The current prison was designated a dispersal prison in 1966. It is now a main lifer centre with the focus on serious sex offenders. The sort that tabloid newspaper readers would like to castrate or kill. And I for one cannot blame them, although I no longer read newspapers.

The average prison roll at Wakeford is approximately 740 including 100 Category A and 10 High Risk Category A prisoners. The sort of guys who almost persuade me that evil exists and is not simply a religious confidence trick.

If I'd gone through the right channels it would have taken forever, and in the end I'd have probably been denied my request. If I visited on Saturdays, there's be little chance of getting the privacy I required. So I had to ask Chief Superintendent Silcock for a letter.

Silcock refused to see me in the police HQ in town. And I was not the sort of person he ought to be seen with socially. A copper has to choose his mates with care. And that applies to the women too, but it had not posed a problem for Sergeant Brigid Riley.

Not for the first time Silcock chose a restaurant well away from the city. A place where we could sit and talk, A place where yobbos were unlikely to visit. That is something the Boers never understood in the old days: there are better strategies than laws to keep people apart. In any case, most people choose to socialise with their own kind. High prices serve as a way of keeping people segregated. Silcock likes his grub and even more he likes it when others are meeting the bill. The people in the *Dog and Partridge,* mostly retired couples who could afford the prices and, fortunately, so could I.

Jack Rubin Associates has been doing quite well recently. My business partner, Mr Mohammed Ali Malik, has a knack of finding work for me to do. What he dislikes, and intensely, is when I do work *pro bono*, without payment.

But this case was not one of those. I had Burnside's cheque. However, as I'd proved Burnside was a liar, I decided that on my return to the office I would check my bank statement on line.

'You mix with some very dubious characters, Jack,' Silcock said.

On entry to the restaurant we had been shown to a small table in a corner, where we could buy drinks and look at the menu. Silcock ordered a soft drink - 'Doctor's orders,' he said. I usually drink cognac but today - as it was luncheon - I opted for a single Armagnac. One reason for my choice is that I like brandy. The other reason was to impress Silcock with my sophistication.

I had just told him why I wanted to get inside Wakeford.

'Austin's a murderer, not a sex offender,' I said.

'Oh well, that makes it OK, doesn't it?' Silcock said with broad sarcasm.

Not many coppers, of whatever rank, have a good line in irony.

I told him I wanted to be alone with Austin Smith.

'His parents have a car of that name when he was born?' Silcock said, and laughed.

'I didn't know there was a make of car called a Smith,' I said.

'Ah, bloody ah,' Silcock whispered.

What I did not tell Silcock was that Elizabeth Riley had failed to find anything about Burnside or Frank Conteh, and what there was about Suleiman Chopdat was all legal, applications to extend his house, a gun licence, that kind of thing.

'I remembered that Austin has a terrific memory bank,' I said. 'Terrific.'

'Did you put him away, Jack?' He paused. 'I think I'll try the pan fried king scallops, with agnolotti pasta, and cream of pea sauce.'

I doubted his quack would approve of that. And still less Silcock's choice of main course, char grilled rib eye steak, cepe and red wine jus.'

'What about you, Jack?' He paused and then said, laughing. 'This isn't a kosher place, is it?'

'Ah, bloody ah,' I whispered.

The waiter, the maître d', sidled over to take our order.

I chose grilled goat's cheese as my starter, and slow cooked lamb for my main course. The last time I had eaten lamb, I had shit thin for a week, but that is better than the other way round.

Music was playing, the sort of thing to appeal to the old fogeys who appeared to be the main luncheon clientèle at the *Dog and Partridge*.

'Good music,' I said to the maître d'.

'Do you like big bands, Sir?' he asked.

'That's Roy Fox and his Band.'

'I'll check the disc,' he said, and went behind a counter.

He returned with the news that it was indeed *Sweet and Lovely* with the Roy Fox band.

'Singer.......Al Bowlly,' I said. 'Recorded in London in.....1931, I think.'

'Where do you get the time to learn all this stuff?' Silcock asked.

'My mother used to sing that to me,' I said. 'Bowlly was a South African.' And I started to sing: 'Sweet and lovely, Sweeter than the roses in May, Sweet and lovely, Heaven must have sent her my way.'

We sat down at our allotted table.

'This singer,' Silcock said.

'Al Bowlly?'

'Was he also a Yid?'

'He was born in Mozambique of Lebanese and Greek parents but he was brought up in Jo'burg,' I said.

Silcock made short work of his scallops.

'Now, why was it you wanted to talk to Austin Smith?' he said.

Chapter Seven

Austin Smith couldn't even claim it had been a crime of passion. A sudden urge. A moment of blind hatred. No! he had planned carefully, and knew exactly when he was going to kill the guy. He also knew where he was going to dump him. A wood sawyer's yard out near Rustenberg.

I'd been assigned the case, mainly because it was cut and dried. Austin refused to enter a plea and did not have defence counsel. There were no kudos in such a case for those higher up the ladder, keen to be promoted.

I think what annoyed the judge, really pissed him off, was that Austin refused to enter a plea. All he said throughout the trial was that his name was Augustine Ignatius Smith. I suppose that with as name like Smith it helps to have a couple of monikers that help you to stand out from the legions of Smiths. He would not look at the judge, or anyone else. Judges don't like that kind of thing. This one gave Austin thirty. Years, that is. It was what he deserved.

Yet, out of court, in his cell, Austin was willing to talk to me. He told me all about the reason he'd planned to kill the guy. It was what the tabloid newspapers call a gangland killing. A turf war.

Shortly after the conclusion of the case, I had quit the force, after false accusation of bribery were levelled at me. At about the same time, Austin Smith had quit human society. The scum he was incarcerated with, the perverts and sickos, can hardly be called human.

I was shown into a small room and had to wait about fifteen minutes before Austin was brought in.

He saw me, looked puzzled, and then remembered who I was.

'Mr Rubin!'

He held out his hand in greeting. A warder restrained him.

We sat opposite each other at a small table. Otherwise, the room was bare.

'How are you, Austin?' I said.

I took his hand and shook it vigorously. The warder did not look happy.

Tough shit!

I asked the warder if I could have privacy with my client. Let him think I was from the legal side.

'I'll be just outside, Sir,' the warder said, 'in case you need any help.'

I resisted the temptation to ask why I should have anything to fear from Austin Smith. After all, he was nothing more dangerous than a cold-blooded, vicious gangster and killer.

Austin's face was covered in bruises and he had a gap in his front teeth.

'The staff did that to you, Austin?' I said.

He grinned. 'No way! One of the other prisoners.'

'Are you having a rough time in here?' I said. 'Some nasty bruises there.'

He grinned again.

You should see the other guy,' he said. 'Or rather, you shouldn't see the other guy.'

'An argument?'

'A new guy. Just transferred here.'

'Do you have to mix with nonces?' I said.

I wasn't sure I'd like to spend any recreational time with child murderers and molesters.

'This guy isn't a nonce. Just a hard man head banger. He decided he wants to be head man in our section. And made sure everybody knew it.' Austin paused. 'And I objected, and we had a.....there was a fight.'

'You lost a tooth,' I said, 'but won the fight. Like that, was it?'

'Bang on, Mr Rubin.'

'You're a tough man,' I said.

'Yeah! But stupid?'

'Stupid?' I said.

'I must be, or I wouldn't be banged up in here, would I?'

It takes an intelligent man to know that he is stupid.

'Now, Austin. I want you to help me, if you can.'

'Sure, Mr Rubin. Anything for a friend.'

That I was not his friend was clear to me, but this wasn't the time to tell him so.

'Frank Conteh,' I said.

Austin looked serious. Rubbed his nose.

'He's a bad guy, Mr Rubin. You watch yourself when you play with Frank.'

'Tell me about him,' I said.

Austin looked at the black ruck sack I'd brought in with me. The guards had checked it carefully but had decided that there was nothing wrong with bringing in two hundred cigarettes. Ten packets of twenty. I passed over one packet. A good brand. Austin produced a match from somewhere - seemed to be the back of his head - and lit up. He exhaled smoke with evident satisfaction. If I face twenty inside, I think I might start smoking again. I too was once a slave to My Lady Nicotine.

'Frank....he's not from round here. I think he's from down South somewhere.'

'What's his racket?'

Drugs, guns, smuggling cigarettes, girls.'

'That's quite a portfolio, Austin,' I said.

'I'd agree with you, Mr Rubin. If I knew what a portfolio was.'

He grinned. The cigarettes were relaxing him.

'Frank has done time,' Austin said.

That had not come up on the police files. Not yet, anyway, but Brigid Riley was no doubt still searching.

'Where did he do his time?'I said.

'I dunno. We was never close, Frank and me.'

Which was Austin's way of saying that Frank Conteh was a competitor, and enemy.

'There was one time.....' Austin was struggling to remember........'he was running guns into Ireland, and then over to this country.'

'Who were the guns for?'

'Anybody'd buy them,' Austin said.

'Anything political?' I said.

'Not that I ever heard.'

I went to the door. Asked the warder if I could have water to drink.

'And Austin?' he asked.

'Why not?'

I went back inside and sat down at the table. Austin was lighting another cigarette.

'Tell me,' I said, 'does Frank Conteh work for himself? Or does he have a Boss?'

'Frank work for himself?' Austin sneered. 'Guys like Frank never work fore themselfs.'

I understood. Conteh not only had muscles on his body, especially his arms, but he had gristle between his ears, where his brain should have been.

'Who is Frank's Boss?' I said.

'It used to be a black guy from Zambia. A guy settled over here. Cosmos. Know him?'

I shook my head. I'd never heard of Cosmos.

The warder came in with two plastic containers. I think they had been used several times already, but at least the water was fresh and cold.

'Used to be?' I said, nudging Austin along.

'Yeah! Cosmos was arrested. Deported to the States.'

'But he came from Zambia.'

'Yeah! But it seems he was wanted in the States.'

'So....with Cosmos across the Pond....who does Frank work for now?'

'Not so fast, Mr Rubin. Remember, I am stupid.'

I drank my water and waited.

'Cosmos came back. Cleared in the USA. But he was killed. And who do you think put him to sleep?'

'Frank Conteh?'

'Right, Mr Rubin, you already knew that.'

I didn't know that but this was no time to let on.

'You guys couldn't pin Frank fore the killing, so they got him on income tax. Frank claimed he had no income so didn't need to pay income tax, but they nailed him for three years, anyway.'

I did not want Frank Conteh's record. I wanted to know who he was currently working for. I had my suspicions.

Austin started to rub his forehead vigorously. He was trying to remember.

'You know, Mr Rubin....I can't remember the guy's name.'

'Maybe you never knew,' I said.

He grinned.

'I keep in touch with the Outside,' he said.

'These cigarettes...the other nine packets. Would they assist your memory, you old rogue?'

'Make me an offer,' he said, grinning, and the gap in his teeth made him look mischievous, rather than the nasty crook he really was.

'Remember the name, and you win two hundred gigs,' I said.

'And if I don't remember?'

'You get the cigs anyway, Austin.'

That pleased him. He wanted to be top man in his section and that meant buying support against the guy seeking to usurp him. With two hundred cigarettes, Austin would be able to purchase a fair amount of support.

He closed his eyes. Like that, and with the bruises, he looked a real ugly brute. Not someone to tangle with.

'I can see the name now. In my mind. It begins with....the letter C.'

'Chopdat,' I said, and could not conceal the triumph from my voice.

'No, not that,' Austin replied.

That brought me back down to earth with a considerable bump.

'The letter C,' I said.

'Coburn!' Austin said, the name exploding from his cracked lips.

'Coburn.'

I passed over the plastic bag containing the cigarettes.

'Alfred Coburn,' Austin said.

He drank his water. He seemed exhausted. All that remembering had sapped his strength.

And now it was time for me to leave. If I stayed much longer, I'd be in danger of becoming institutionalised.

I stood up. Shook Austin's hand again.

'Augustine Ignatius Smith,' I said, 'you are a star.'

I called for the warder, standing outside, earwigging.

'I have given two hundred cigarettes to this prisoner,' I said. 'As an unsolicited gift.'

The warder leaned over to take the bag. He proceeded to pour out the packets.

'What did you do that for?' I said.

'We don't want Mr Smith to put the bag over his heads and top himself, now do we?' the man asked with heavy irony.

Like I have said, law enforcement personnel don't do irony. Not very well, anyway.

'There is one other thing, Mr Rubin,' Austin said, grabbing at my sleeve. 'Conteh. That isn't Frank's real name.'

'What is it? His real name?'

'I don't know,' he said.

'Come on, Austin. Try to remember,' I said.

'I can't remember, Mr Rubin. Because I never knew, did I? What I never knew, I can't remember, can I?'

As I walked out of the prison gates, and into bright sunshine, I felt very pleased that I was not a prisoner, incarcerated for years with head bangers and nonces. If I were in such a situation I'd be using the first plastic bag I could get my hands on.

Chapter Eight

Malik was hunched over the computer in the office.

"It's cleared,' he said, and thumped the table.

I switched on the Morphy Richards.

Malik was checking our business account online. Burnside's cheque had cleared and we were four grand better off. This was a time for celebration, which, that early in the morning, meant a pot of lemon and ginger tea. Camomile to calm me down, lemon and ginger to pep me up. I need neither, if truth be told, but I do enjoy tea.

'We can eat out at lunch time,' Malik said.

'Not me,' I said. 'I have to earn that four grand, remember?'

'So what is your next move, Mr Rubin?'

He always calls me Mister. And he rarely uses short forms. His spoken English is quite formal most of the time. He never cusses or swears oaths either. He is quite the decent family man. Which I am not.

'My next move is to find Coburn,' I said.

'That should not be difficult,' Malik replied.

'I'll probably have him in the bag by the end of today,' I said, feeling cocky.

I sipped my hot tea.

Malik made coffee for himself.

There are two rules in this office: each makes his own beverages; and we never discuss religion.

'I'm going out, Malik,' I said.

'Where are we going, Mr Rubin?'

'*We*, I said, with emphasis, '*we* are going nowhere. I'm going alone.'

This news did not make him glad.

'Just routine stuff,' I said. 'I need to talk to that little shit Ken Gee again.'

'The one with the face like a weasel?'

'Or a ferret,' I said.

'Isn't a weasel and a ferret the same animal?' Malik asked.

'No, a ferret is a domesticated polecat. A stoat and an ermine are the same animal. That's what you're thinking. A stoat is called an ermine when it's coat becomes white in Winter.'

'You know a lot of things, Mr Rubin,' Malik said and his eyes were a mixture of admiration and envy.

'That's because I read a lot. And I went to a good school.'

'Where they taught you to use bad language.'

'Do you know, Malik,' I said, 'I never swore till I met you.'

When I found Ken Gee he was on a street corner outside a snooker club, arguing with two uniformed coppers. The little ferret - weasel or stoat, never ermine, not even in Winter - was loudly proclaiming that he had his human rights. A crowd had gathered, as always happens when there's excitement.

I pushed my way through and spoke to a uniform. He did not know me - why should he? - and didn't quibble when I said that Ken Gee was one of my informers and I needed to talk to him urgently.

Neither copper asked to see my credentials; they even referred to me as 'Sir'. I took hold of Ken Gee and dragged him down the street, to jeers from the crowd.

Once we were round a corner, and had found a bit of quiet, Ken Gee started to tell me his thoughts about policemen, and stuttered something about what pigs they were, and he had his 'yooman rights.'

'Shut up, Ken,' I said, 'or I'll give you a good hiding. Savvy?'

The weasel savvied okay.

We went to a small coffee bar. A greasy spoon I'd not usually grace with my presence and my money, but Ken was at home in such a place.

I ordered two coffees and biscuits. I even purchased a packet of cheap cigs for Ken. Except these days no brand of cigarettes can be called cheap.

'Right, Ken....'

'Yes, Mr Rubin.'

Maybe he thought I was going to dole out money on top of the cigarettes and the coffee.

'What's new on the street about Frank Conteh?'

His eyes narrowed. 'So you've heard.'

'Tell me in your own words, Ken,' I said, as if I knew what he was talking about.

'It's new,' he said.

'How new is new?'

I heard it this morning,' he said.

Which did not mean anything; it could have been old hat, but new to him. After all, in the sea that is life, Ken Gee is a bottom feeder, a loser of no status whatsoever.

'They're saying' - he looked furtively round the café and lowered his voice to a barely audible whisper - 'they're saying Frank killed a guy.'

I was interested.

'Who did you hear it from, Kenneth?'

'Charlie. My neighbour.'

'Charlie?'

'Simmonite.'

'And Charlie Simmonite casually walked over to the broken fence that separates your two gardens and gave you this news?'

'We were in Mike's.'

'The shack that does breakfasts for truckers?'

'That's right,' Ken said. 'You get a good cheap breakfast at Mike's.'

'And what does this Charlie Simmonite do for a living?'

'He drives a taxi, innit?'

'I'll check him on the list,' I said, meaning the register of taxi drivers maintained down at the Civil Centre.

'He's not registered,' Ken said quickly.

That did not surprise me. Mr Simmonite ran an illegal taxi service and also claimed benefits. The takings from the taxi business were all in cash and never saw a bank account, or were divulged to HMRC, as the tax man is known these days.

'Charlie takes on any job that brings in the loot,' Ken said.

He thinks that kind of talk makes him tough. Yet you only have to look at him, the thin weasel face, the baggy trousers with a low arse, and you can tell he's as soft as shit. But I have to give him this - the little bugger keeps his ear to the ground.

'He doesn't ask questions. Well, it seems he was called to pick up this guy. It was Frank. And Charlie drove him round the city. It lasted all evening. Seemed money was no object.'

'Frank was looking for somewhere?Or someone?'

'Right, Jack,' Ken said, and I decided to let it pass, that he had called me by my first name.

'Tell me more, Ken,' I said.

'Frank was in a state of excitement and anger. Charlie was shit scared. He just had to cruise round the streets, checking out girls. When they saw one, or a group, Charlie had to drive slow, like.'

'As if they were pavement crawlers,' I said.

'Yeah! Frank checked a lot of girls but didn't find the particular one he was searching for.'

'These girls. Did Charlie tell you that Frank was looking for a particular type of girl?'

'What do you mean?' Ken asked.

'Frank is black, right?'

'Yeah.'

'Was he only checking black girls? Or only white girls?'

'He was searchin' for one particular girl, like I told you.'

'So you did,' I said.

I ordered two more coffees and biscuits. I'd scoffed the biscuits in the first round.

I sat down again. I tossed a twenty note across the table. Ken Gee's eyes lit up.

'Very interesting, Ken,' I said, 'very interesting indeed.'

I swallowed the coffee hastily. It tasted like witch piss, and no amount of sugar could disguise the taste. Ken seemed to be enjoying his.

I sat down on a bench in the Market Place The bench was made of solid concrete, never friendly to human flesh. I noted that it was fastened securely into the ground. No rioters were ever going to uproot that and throw it around.

I dialled Brigid's cell phone. She'd forbidden me to contact her in the office.

'Hello?'

'Sergeant Riley?'

There was a short silence.

'Jack?'

'Hi!' I said.

I rarely use such a greeting but it seemed right for Brigid at that moment.

'What have you got for me, Bridge?'

'Nothing on Burnside. Plenty on Conteh. Nothing on the girl.'

'Thanks. For trying, I mean.' I paused. 'When are you next off duty?'

'Not for ten days.'

'Then I'll call you,' I said. 'Take you away for a sexy weekend.'

'And I, Sir, might just agree to go with you.'

It wasn't far to the office. Malik was sitting there, surfing the Net, looking miserable.'

'Why such a long face, Malik?' I said. 'When we've just deposited money into the account.'

'It's the way you stop.....prevent me from knowing what's going on.'

'I want to protect you from danger, Malik. It's a dangerous and wicked world out there on the streets,' I said.

'Sure!' Malik said. 'And who protects you, Mr Rubin? Eh? Who protects you?'

Chapter Nine

Finding Charlie Simmonite proved to be easy. I asked round the taxi rank outside the railway station.

Nobody wanted to talk to me. Not until I made it clear I was willing to pay for information. Money loosens tongues around the world.

The guy who eventually took me to one side was a middle-aged Sikh. At least, I think he was middle-aged: with all that hair under his turban, fine moustaches and an uncut beard, he could have been younger. He was no friend of Charlie's.

'That man! He creeps in the town. He steals food from our mouths.'

And he whispered that Charlie was not an honest man, but I was not to quote him.

I asked in which ways Charlie Simmonite was dishonest.

'He works with gangsters,' the Sikh said.

I questioned him further but he was not forthcoming with details. He works with gangsters was not much use to me. I had worked out that possibility already. But one comment was.

'That man, he works for many days and then he.....he seems to disappear.'

'What motor does he run?'

'An old Cortina,' the man told me. 'But I saw him one day in a BMW, black, new model.'

I slipped a twenty note to the taxi driver. Never was money more easily earned.

The sun was shining. I strolled across the square and down to the open market, an old attractive building now dwarfed by a Tesco supermarket whose architect must have been a seven year old kid with partial sight.

I bought an orange. It would have been cheaper to fly a budget airline to Israel and picked my own fruit from the tree. I peeled the orange slowly. Pigeons flew at me from all directions. They were wasting their time; I don't throw litter and peelings on to the streets.

Charlie Simmonite was a pirate taxi driver. He needed to work regularly and often, but he took time off, often many days. That meant that he was either an idle sod, who had to stay at home and gather his strength. or he had other onions to fry as well as driving an unregistered taxi.

I walked back to Station Square by way of two back streets. It was my lucky day. As I was walking toward the rank outside the station, I noticed an old battered Cortina outside the Head of Steam. This used to be the first-class waiting room of the railway station but is now a boozer that sells food. Not the kind of food that I like to eat. The driver of the Cortina was away from the other taxis, but was, it seemed to me, waiting.

'You a taxi?' I asked.

'Yeah. Get in.'

He drove away quickly. Did not want to be observed too closely by the Punjabi chapter of the taxi association.

'Where to, mate?'

'Temple Street, Newlands,' I said. 'Do you know it?'

The man grinned.

'Know it? I live there, don't I?'

I looked for a meter but there wasn't one. This didn't surprise me.

Temple Street was where Ken Gee lived and he had claimed Charlie Simmonite was a neighbour.

It took less than ten minutes to reach our destination.

'What number, mate?'

'Your place, Charlie,' I said.

He slammed on the anchors but didn't switch off the engine.

'Yer what?'

'You heard me, Charlie,' I said. 'Let's talk at your place.'

'You the fuzz?' Charlie said.

'Are you Charlie Simmonite?'

'Yer.'

'Then I'm the fuzz,' I said. And added, firmly: 'Your place, Charlie.'

He drove round the back of a row of terraced houses and into a back yard from which all evidence of grass and soil had been removed. There was space for three cars.

Charlie switched off the engine.

'Look, Mister -'

'Rubin. Chief Inspector Rubin.'

'I can explain,' he said.

'I'm not concerned about your being a pirate taxi, Charles,' I said.

'My mates call me Charlie,' he said.

'Is that a fact, Charles? Well, I'm not your mate. OK? But you are going to talk to me.'

It was warm in the Cortina, even with the windows open. The stink of Charlie's sweat did not help me to feel comfortable.

'Let's go inside,' I said.

'We can't. The wife's there,' he protested.

I checked the yard.

'Then we'll sit on the back step, in the shade.'

The noise of two doors banging brought a woman to the door. Her sort can be seen often in Newlands. Just one step above slattern.

Charlie asked me if I wanted a beer. I declined the offer. Said I wanted cold water. Charlie went inside the house. Came back empty-handed.

He sat down and looked at me expectantly. Before I had time to speak, Charlie's wife, or maybe partner - one can never be sure, these days - emerged with a bottle of lager and a glass of water. No words were uttered, apart from my Thank You.

'What's this about, Mr Rubin?' Charlie asked, his voice a mixture of fear and bravado, with fear uppermost.

I examined my glass. It was not the cleanest glass I've ever been given, but not the dirtiest, either. The dirtiest was at Cairo Airport, when I was unloading Egyptian pounds prior to escaping to the cleanliness of Zurich.

'I'm not with the local force,' I said. 'I'm not interested in your being a pirate taxi and claiming benefits at the same time.'

'I gotta claim. I got a wife and kids,' he said.

'Just shut up, Charlie, and listen,' I said sternly.

Charlie buttoned his lip..

I took out my wallet and extracted the photograph of Jessica.

'Do you know this woman?' I said.

His mouth was round the neck of the beer bottle. He peered intently at the photo.

'She's a good-looking kid,' Charlie said.

That wasn't what I had asked him but I did not blame him for noticing that Jessica Connelly was a stunner. After all, that had been my first response when Burnside had showed me the pic.

'Where do I find her, Charlie?' I said, leaning in to him, despite the stink of his sweat-soaked tee-shirt.

'Honest, Mr Rubin. I never seen her before.' He paused. 'But I'd like to.'

He grinned, displaying a set of dirty stained teeth. This guy could have been Ken Gee's brother, they both had the same verminous look.

'OK, let's move on, Charlie. Let's talk about Big Frank?'

'Who?'

His question came out rather too fast. He knew damn well who Frank Conteh was.

'The big black gangster with the muscles,' I said. 'The guy you drove round time looking for a certain woman.'

I pretended to laugh with disbelief.

'The last guy who lied to me,' I said, keeping my voice soft and menacing, 'finished up with a dislocated shoulder and a broken knee bone.'

'I drive taxis. I have as lot of customers,' Charlie said.

There was even more sweat on his face. He wiped his forehead with the back of his hand. Guys like Charlie can dish it out but threaten them back with rough stuff and they start to shit themselves.

He shouted: 'Same again, Coll.'

'Coll?'

'Colleen,' he said.

'How many kids, Charlie?'

'Three. With Coll, that is.'

The little *mamzer* had probably been spreading his seed since about the age of fifteen. And he was paid generously for it by stupid tax payers like me.

The lovely Colleen, hair unwashed, hanging down like rats' tails, skin blemished and in need of sunshine, came out with another beer. She took my empty glass, never said a word. I heard the tap water, and then she returned with the full glass.

Once the delectable Colleen had returned to her domestic chores, or maybe some shitty daytime TV show, because I could hear the voices of a TV set, I leaned in to Charlie Simmonite again.

'You were seen, Charlie,' I said.

'Seen?'

'CCTV. Witnesses.'

'I was jus' drivin' this black guy.'

'Two jobs, Charlie. Two post offices.'

The sweat rolling down his face was a positive Niagara.

'One in Birch Hill. One over in Brigston. A big black guy, Frank, with a hand gun and a....you behind the wheel, Charlie. You were seen.'

My voice was barely more than a whisper. I learned that from Brando in the *Godfather* movie.

Just when he was about to break, weeping, sweating profusely, ready to spill his guts, blaming everything on Big Frank, Colleen came to the door.

'You're wanted, Charlie,' she said. 'At the front door.'

71

'Tell him 'm busy,' Charlie said roughly.

'It's the post man. He needs a signature,' Colleen said.

Charlie stood up and I did the same. I held out my hand, took his car keys from him.

Charlie went inside. These terraced houses have a front door and one at the back.

I put the photograph of Jessica back in my wallet.

Then I heard a shrill cry that turned into as scream. I confess I did not move quickly. Women like Colleen like to weep and wail. But when she became shriller still, and it was clear her grief was genuine, I went inside.

Colleen was in the poor excuse for a front garden. She was spread over the body of Charlie Simmonite. He was bleeding. I had not heard the shots. Gun fire is not loud like you hear in the movies and on TV. But someone had plugged Charlie with two bullets, one in his chest, one in his face. Or what had once been a face but was now a bloody mess of tangled flesh and bone.

Chapter Ten

The office is in one of those modern skyscrapers that are appearing even in our provincial towns and cities, this one constructed on the riverside.

There was a security guard, trying to look important behind a shining new desk. I was asked to state my business. I was instructed to sign my name in a visitors' book and write down the purpose of my visit and the registration number of my motor vehicle.

'Would you also like the maiden name of my mother?' I said, stroppy.

'That won't be necessary, Sir,' the security man said.

He pointed to the lifts.

'Fourth floor,' he said.

'I'll climb the steps,' I said, determined to be difficult.

'You'll please yourself.'

I hate this kind of functionary. In fact, I hate all functionaries. They don't bring out the best in me.

I turned away, stopped and looked back.

'Esther Hagar,' I said.

'Sir?'

'My mother's maiden name,' I said.

It was obvious that he would have liked to have hit me, hard, and thrown me out in the street. Well, if he had been so foolish, he would have been making a big mistake.

I also made a mistake, climbing four flights of steps. By the time I reached the fourth floor I was in a lather, and that despite the air con.

I dried my face with a handkerchief, composed myself, and found a door with a slide-in name plate. Number 4, Coburn: Imports and Exports. In small letters, so as to fit in the plate. Difficult to read. But at least Brigid Riley had found the right office.

'Good morning,' I said.

The woman looked up at me, suspicion in her eyes, or so I interpreted that owlish stare.

'I'd like to see Mr Coburn,' I said. 'Alfred Coburn.'

'Do you have an appointment, Mr...er....'

'Rubin,' I said. 'Jack Rubin.'

'Do you have an appointment, Mr Rubin?'

'No, but I think he'll agree to see me.'

'Mr Coburn only sees people by appointment,' the shrew said.

OK, she'd transmuted from an owl to a shrew in a short space of time.

'Tell him my name is Chief Inspector Rubin. Tell him I'm assisting his friend Mr Burnside in an investigation.'

'Assisting?' she asked quietly.

'A missing person case,' I said.

The shrew was making notes.

'I don't think Mr Coburn is going to change his rules, just for you.'

'Rules?'

'About never seeing anyone who doesn't have an appointment.'

'Not even the police?' I said.

'He has never had a visit from a police officer before, Mr Rubin.'

She stood up. Behind her was a door, no doubt the entrance to the private office of Alfred Coburn, who could not possibly break his rules, not even for a ranking copper. Between me and that door was the reception desk.

'Wait here and I'll see what he says,' she ordered, unsmiling, 'but I cannot say that I am very optimistic.'

Her back view was neat enough, nice arse, but not nice enough to compensate for her face and her manner.

I looked round the waiting area. What is it, I asked myself, while I waited for the shrew to return, that they have to keep secret? It is probably easier to get into the Bank of England or Fort Knox.

Brigid had told me Coburn claimed to import and export many different goods and items - agricultural machinery, sewing machines, cloth, foodstuffs.

On the wall there was an old photograph of when tram cars used to run in the streets outside. One photograph, and the rest, like the old woman's cupboard, was bare. Not even a chair for a weary visitor to rest his weary bones on. Even the shrew's worktop did not seem the place for a busy woman. No sign of a laptop, no files, just a telephone. There was a sign saying *No Smoking*. When I see such a sign, I crave a cigarette, just to be bolshie.

The woman returned. If anything, her face was more sad than before.

'I'm sorry, Mr....er....'

The bitch was pretending she couldn't remember my name, although she had written in her pad, the one still in her left hand.

'Chief Inspector Rubin,' I said, lying through my thirty-two teeth.

'I'm sorry, Mr Rubin, but Mr Coburn cannot see you. He has instructed me to get you to make an appointment.'

'Is that what he really said?'

I smiled a little, to put her off guard.

'If you'll give me your details, and the reason you want to -'

'Cut the crap!' I said savagely, cutting in.

'Sir?'

'Tell Coburn I want to see him now, right now,' I said.

'But he's not available,' she replied.

I leaned over the desk.

'Then...... you tell him to make himself available. Now now!'

'But that's not possible.'

'If you don't get in there, I'm going to rip off that blouse and tie your tits in a knot round your neck. That clear enough, baby?'

She wasted no time retreating to the inner office.

I nosed around. Under the counter was a paperback book. A romance. The front cover showed a handsome rich man lounging next to a Lexus, and looking at him, in clear adoration, a young woman - his secretary, or PR assistant.

Perhaps the sour shrew imagined herself as the young girl, and Alfred Coburn as her lover.

She came back, closed the door behind her. She seemed composed enough, in spite of what I'd threatened to do to her.

She cleared her throat.

'I'm sorry, Sir, but it's impossible.'

'Nothing is impossible,' I said.

I moved to the door.

She stood in my way.

'Look,' I said, putting my face close to hers. 'I don't like to strike a women, but if you don't shift your arse -'

I must have sounded convincing. She stepped smartly to one side.

I walked through to the inner office. There was no one there. There was a single desk and a chair but nothing on the desk. No computer, no telephone, nothing.

There were three doors leading out. The first, I'd just come through. I opened the second door. It was a toilet. There was no one sitting on the bog, no one washing his hands hygienically. The third door, which I opened confidently, was into another office. This too was a small office, with a desk and a black office chair. On the desk was a computer, mouse, the whole shebang, connected to the Internet, and a telephone receiver. There was also an ash tray. I sniffed. Whoever had been working at this desk had been smoking, and only recently, for not only was there the stink of cigarette smoke, but someone had stubbed out a cigarette, and in some haste, for it was still burning.

Coburn had been there, smoking, only minutes earlier. His secretary had kept me talking until he had a chance to escape. I tried to open the door. It was locked. Coburn was slowing me down.

I rushed back to the reception area and the secretary with the neat arse and a shrewish face. She'd lead me to Coburn. But she was not there either. Another swift departure, a vanishing act.

She could not have gone far; was probably still in the lift going down. I turned the door handle. No dice. That was locked too. Clever, clever. I was locked in the office. No windows. Doors that would not give easily. This wasn't the movies, where doors give easily to a single heroic shoulder charge.

I checked the other door, just to be sure. Still locked. I wondered for a while what to do. There must be an alarm system or something. There was nothing. I began to fear I was going to be locked in here for some time, maybe all night, and I began to experience the fears of claustrophobia.

Then I started to laugh. And I spoke aloud.

'Rubin! You stupid pillock!'

I picked up the telephone receiver and called the office. Malik answered immediately.

'Any calls for me?' I asked gaily.

'Just the tart,' Malik said.

'The tart?'

'Your police sergeant pal,' he said.

'Oh good,' I said, and then added, 'Malik, do me a favour.'

I told him where I was.

'Get a locksmith round here, right now.'

'A locksmith?' he said, like the parrot he sometimes is. 'Why do you want a locksmith?'

'Because I'm locked in, that's why,' I said. 'Coburn. He's a shifty swine.'

Chapter Eleven

The afternoon remained warm, and warm into early evening.

I walked back to the office, with Malik walking jubilantly beside me. Jubilant because he'd had to rescue me. He had not found a locksmith. He'd simply walked into the building and asked the Security guy to provide a duplicate key, which he duly did.

OK, OK, so I had not thought of ringing down to the ground-floor reception. So.....nobody's perfect, and certainly not Jack Rubin, and Malik was having fun reminding me of that fact.

I phoned Brigid. She was proving to be a star. She had found details of where Coburn lived. From the tax records of the local authority. It seemed that Coburn paid local tax for two properties: one a large house, Band A, in Beaumont Park, the upmarket part; and a flat in a block of apartments in the town centre.

Malik did not seem in any mood to go home, and neither did I. I suggested that we check out the apartment. It was not far from where Coburn had an office, and he'd probably chosen to go there. Whether or not accompanied by the shrew, I did not know, and I didn't give a damn either.

We walked along the grid, and then down a side street toward the Public Library and Art Gallery.

It was warm and pleasant at that time of the late afternoon, and walking is always a good exercise. Malik needs to lose weight, swears he will do so very soon, and never does. He likes Mona's cooking too much.

We arrived at the block of flats. It was a gated development, as they usually are nowadays. Brigid had provided the necessary details. I peered at the names and numbers outside. But I did not see the name A Coburn. No, in S4/32 the name was - and no way was I surprised - that of R. Connelly.

Coburn was not the first guy to pay for a flat for his girl friend, and he won't be the last, either. I knew he paid the taxes and probably the rent too. Chances were he met the expenses for utilities too. And clothing, shoes, TV, entertainment. He could afford it from his import and export business, whatever that entailed.

I rang the buzzer for S4/32. Flat number thirty-two on the fourth floor. I hoped there would be a lift. I'd had enough of steps for one day. I pressed hard and kept pressing. There was no answer. The lovely Jessica was either out - she enjoyed dancing, Burnside had said - or her TV was on so loud she could not hear that she had visitors.

'Buzz the caretaker,' Malik suggested.

He'd found the number at the bottom. In case of emergency ring etc etc.

'Good thinking, Batman,' I said.

The caretaker answered. He sounded sleepy. Perhaps he'd nodded off after a busy day. I cannot say I would have blamed him, so intense had the heat been for about four weeks now.

'Who is it?'

'I need to get to S4/32,' I said.

'Why?'

He seemed to be an uncivil git, like our own caretaker in Station Chambers. Maybe all caretakers are like that. Maybe it is part of the job description. *Wanted Caretaker. Must be a grumpy old git.*

'Police,' I said.

Malik gave me a look.

'Wha'?' the caretaker said.

'Police. Open up.'

'Give your name and rank,' old grumpy said.

Grumpy he might have been but he was also crafty.

I did not hesitate.

'Rubin. Chief Inspector.'

There was a whirr of electricity. We were over the first hurdle.

We climbed the steps slowly. No way did I want to arrive at the top in a lather, fighting for breath when I confronted Coburn or Jessica, or, as I hoped, both of them together.

The caretaker, a white guy, was waiting for us. He was a tall scruffy man, with a slight stoop.

Malik shook his hand. Malik always shakes hands. I was glad to see the man standing there; it meant he wasn't on the telephone, checking me out with Central.

'Nobody's answering number thirty-two,' I said, lying, because we had not tried that number, wanting the element of surprise to work for us.

The person who has surprise on his side, starts at a great advantage. I secretly hoped that Coburn and Jessica could be caught *in flagrante delicto* - red-handed, in the act of sexual congress, as they say in the courts of law. In that case, red-handed is hardly the best description.

I signalled to Malik. He knocked on the door. Several times, louder each knock. I expected a neighbour to emerge and ask what the hell the noise was all about.

'There's nobody in,' the caretaker said, stating the obvious. Except he was wrong.

'Tell me about the girl.'

'Girl?'

He really was an obtuse bugger, slow as a snail.

'Jessica Connelly. That lives in this flat,' I said.

Malik had stopped knocking.

'Never seen her,' the caretaker said, picking his nose.

'And Mr Coburn, who pays for everything?'

'Nothing to do with me. That's the owners,' he said.

'Where is your duplicate?' Malik asked.

He gave me a look and a half-smile. Malik knew all about duplicate keys.

On the caretaker's broad belt there was an assortment of keys. They must have weighed a bit. Perhaps that stoop was an inguinal hernia.

By this time my nose was beginning to twitch. There was a definite smell. I caught Malik's eye and he nodded slightly - he'd also noticed the niff.

'Give me the key and stand back,' I said to the caretaker.

He did as ordered. I turned the key and opened the door.

'Christ!' the caretaker said, taking a couple of steps away from the door.

The smell hit me hard too. I placed my handkerchief over my nose and mouth, but it wasn't much of a barrier.

The apartment had a lounge, kitchen area, and two bedrooms. The dead body was on the floor in one of the bedrooms. He had been stabbed several times.

'You can wait outside, Mr Malik,' I said gently.

He shook his head but did not speak. Didn't want that most awful of stinks to enter his mouth.

Flies were buzzing in that bedroom, going frantic. They always do when there's dead flesh, whether it's a mouse, a rat or, as in this case, a man.

'Shit!' Malik said, which is as near as I have ever heard him cuss.

'Worse than shit,' I said, waving my arms to brush away the flies, which refused to be brushed away.

Malik's sallow face had turned a pale shade of green, like a lettuce about to give up the ghost.

'Open the windows,' I said.

He did as commanded, while I gingerly examined the man's body.

When he returned to the bedroom, Malik asked,

'How long has he been dead, Mr Rubin?'

'I'm no expert. But I'd say - at a guess - between four and ten days. There's putrefaction. The stink is the smell of methane and hydrogen sulphide.'

'Rotten eggs,' Malik said.

'He's still bloated. Black putrefaction hasn't set in yet.' I brushed away flies as best I could. 'I learned this when I was a young copper.'

'Let's get out of here, Mr Rubin,' Malik said.

On the landing there was no sign of the caretaker. Malik retched several times but did not vomit.

I could have used a long shower and a gallon of mouth wash.

I heard the sound of a klaxon horn. The caretaker had telephoned for an ambulance or maybe the police.

I dashed back into the flat. In the bedroom I looked again at the bloated stinking body.

I checked the pockets of the dead man's suit. There was a wallet. I wrapped it in my handkerchief.

In a drawer of the bedside locker was a photograph album. I stuck that under my coat.

Malik was shaking. No blame attached.

'Let's get out of here,' I said, 'before the cavalry arrives.'

Back in the office, Malik immediately switched on the kettle. A pot of tea would help immensely.

I checked the wallet. There were photographs. One was of a pretty girl, aged about sixteen - could have been that bit younger - with a middle-aged white guy. Two more snaps of the same girl, a few years older, and more beautiful now that her face was better formed. I turned the photos over. On the back of one there was a written inscription.

'With love, Alfred, From your very own Jess.'

I passed the pictures to Malik.

'There is one beautiful girl,' I said.

My tea made, I drank to slake my thirst and remove the stink of death from my mouth.

'So the dead guy was Coburn,' Malik said.

'Right! Which poses the question, my friend......'

'Yes?'

'Who was the guy in the office earlier today? The one who was in such a hurry to get away.'

Chapter Twelve

I told Malik I was going to drive straight home. I needed a shower and I had to wash all my clothes, to get rid of that stink of putrescence.

Little wonder we try to bury the dead within three days. Who wants to have the final memory of a loved one as a stink in the nostrils?

Not that I believe in love or any of that stuff. My mother is still alive, if you can call advanced senility living. My memories of her are already sullied by images of how she is now, when I'd prefer to remember her as she was when she was younger and healthy. For far too many people this is the way the world ends - not with a bang, but a whimper. For Coburn it had been a blade that put his light out.

I was tired, dirty and hungry. Not a good combination. My stay in the shower was a long stay. I had more than a smell to remove. Perhaps I was trying to scrub away the memory.

It didn't take me long to prepare food. A couple of large potatoes put in the microwave oven for ten minutes and then cut open and margarine inserted. My hunger partially assuaged, I was able to take time lightly frying onions and mushrooms. To these I added black pudding. A couple of eggs whisked in a small bowl and then poured over the onions, mushrooms and black pudding and very soon I had an omelette that would have cost me a pile of bucks in a decent restaurant.

Fortified, clean, the next thing for me was to write some notes. I sat down at the computer and wrote everything down from the moment Mr Burnside had burst into my office to the moment I found Coburn's dead body in an advanced state of decay. So why did I write everything down, even in minute detail? I'll tell you why. It's impossible to remember every details so sometimes it pays to keep a record. The main reason, though, and I readily admit it, was in case some swine decided to knock me off, as they had done Charlie Simmonite and now Alfred Coburn.

This case was becoming a pile of deep shit. What had been a simple search for a good-looking bird had now become two cases of murder. Two that I knew of, that is.

I was pleased that Burnside's money was safely in the bank account of Jack Rubin, Associates. If I'd known my life was going to be in danger, I'd have asked for considerably more in payment.

The next item on the agenda was to confront Frank Conteh. There was no doubt in my mind that he had killed Coburn. Knives were Frank's M.O., his *modus operandi*.

Whether or not he'd bumped off Charlie Simmonite - well, I was less sure of that, but it seemed reasonable to assume he had.

Find Frank Conteh, and you find Jessica. That's what Burnside had said.

I had to find three people: Frank, Jessica and that two-faced rat called Burnside. That Burnside was up to his elbows in shit, I didn't doubt. My one certainty was that Frank was a killer.

'Thrice is he armed that hath his quarrel just, And four times he who gets his blow in fust.'

I was going to get my blow in fust.

In the bedroom there is a large old wardrobe. It may be made of oak. I've never bothered to find out, The reason being, I don't care a toss about such trivia.

I keep the wardrobe locked. Not that it would make a difference is a burglar broke it. Stuck out here in the boonies, as I am, he could smash the furniture with an axe, play *Carmina Burana* at full volume, and nobody would hear.

Inside the wardrobe, hidden under an assortment of clothes, I keep a metal box. This has a double lock and, while not completely secure, would take time to open, and thieves are usually pressed for time. Thus far, I've had no problem with thieves.

I placed the box on the bed. Inside it a gun. It is a Browning. It is protected by soft cloths. Only rarely do I take it out. I am not one of those inadequate pillocks who can only get an erection by looking at gun sites on the web.

The gun is the Browning 1935 FN. sometimes called the Hi-Power. With Frank Conteh loose on the streets and probably looking for me, I had a feeling I might have a use for my Browning. Killing isn't my MO. My gun is for self-defence.

The 1935 FN is the last gun that Browning patented. Apart from the Colt, this is the most successful hand gun ever manufactured. I like it because it is simple and easy to use, and because it fits easily in my pocket. Never in my trouser pocket. That is one accident I want to avoid. A bullet too far. On the other hand, I'm not too keen on a belt holster or a shoulder harness, so the best place is the pocket of my jacket. But, as I say, the number of times I take the gun out means I don't have to worry myself with holsters and harnesses.

The gun is short and lightweight. I can strip it down to six essential parts in a matter of minutes, and I am no engineer, let alone a gunsmith. The gun is reliable and accurate. If you take care of it, that is. I take care of mine. Stripping it down and cleaning the parts beats watching the rubbish on TV any time of the week. Or would do, if I had a television.

It takes most standard ammunition. The magazine holds thirteen shots and there's one carried in the breech. The FN, in case you care, stands for Fabrique National, the Belgian firm.

I'm not going to waste time by talking about trigger guards, anti-rust, or oil. Just to say that when I finally completed the tasks, and replaced the gun in its metal container, I ignored one important rule. I left one 9 mm shell in the breech. It pays, as the Scouts used to say - and may still say for all I know - to be prepared.

There I was, asleep in my bed, and round about dawn, just when I'm dreaming of police sirens, I awake to find blue lights flashing through the curtains, sirens wailing, and noisy buggers breaking down the front door. The next thing I know I am being kicked and punched. Whatever happened to community policing and a duty of care?

I regained full consciousness to find myself on the kitchen floor in the foetal position. It doesn't ward off all blows but it helps to protect the vulnerable soft tissues.

'Get yourself organised, Rubin,' a man in civilian clothes said.

'I tried to sit up.

'Detective Sergeant David Lunn,' I said. 'How are you, Davy?'

Lunn strode forward, boot raised. I was going to receive one hell of a kick. Except I did not relish that prospect. I caught hold of his lower leg, twisted and pushed Lunn back.

One young copper, anxious to assist, came toward me. He wasn't about to hand me a leaflet telling me of the latest deals from Burger King.

'No!' Lunn barked.

He stood up. He needed a bit of effort to achieve this. David Lunn has put on weight since the days when we both joined the Force as young coppers.

'No!' he said again, with more intensity. 'This yid is mine.'

I decided it would be better if I too were on my feet.

Although in civilian clothes, Lunn was armed with a baton.

'You've got this comin' to you, you lousy Jewish yid,' he said, low and mean.

I'm not a Jew but this was no time for a discussion of the subject of what makes a Jew a Jew, and when a Jew is an atheist, and in any case you can't convince these people, Rotten Nazi bigots like Dave Lunn.

I was wearing only my pyjamas.

'Good job I'm not wearing my baby doll nightie, Dave,' I said.

One of the two constables smiled.

We circled each other warily. Lunn had decided that a frontal assault might not be wise. He kept smacking the palm of his left hand with the baton. I know these weapons. They are manufactured from carbon steel. Not something I want across my shoulders or my head. The two coppers had moved back. This is usually the case where people are fighting. I've noticed it before.

Lunn was afraid to come in close. He needed the protection of the baton. Although I had been awakened from a deep sleep, I was now fully alert.

The circling continued. If this had been a prize fight the crowd would by now be baying for action. Or their money back.

Sweat was pouring from Lunn's forehead and the scrap had hardly begun. I guessed that by now he was wishing he could call on the constables for assistance. The only thing stopping him was pride, which goes before destruction. In case you thought it went before a fall, that's a haughty spirit.

Finally, Lunn chanced his arm. He came in closer. I hit him full on the nose. He fell back, spilling blood on my floor. He came again, and I struck him a smart blow on the heart. His face contorted. He fell back. I moved in fast and wrested the baton from his grip.

Then I stepped back. Looked at the young coppers.

'Take it easy, lads,' I said. 'This is an old grudge. From when we both joined the force.'

I slid an upright chair over to Lunn.

'Sit down, Dave,' I said. 'Let's talk this over sensibly.'

I was amazed when he agreed.

'You've got to come in,' Lunn said.

'I will. And tell Mr Silcock all I know. And the Big Dick too.'

The coppers' eyes opened wide. The name - or at least the nickname - of the Chief was enough to awe these young lads.

'Do you want a drink, Dave?' I said amiably.

'On your bike,' Lunn said.

'I'll just get dressed,' I said.

I returned his baton to him and, without waiting for permission, went to the bedroom.

Dressed in casual clothes, I made a last check of the wardrobe. It was locked. I had to take the chance that the police would not pull my house apart later on and find the Browning.

As I left the bedroom, turning to close the door, I felt a heavy pain in my shoulder. That slimy swine Lunn had laid one on me with his steel baton.

I refused to go down. The coppers cuffed me.

Lunn pushed me up against a wall.

'Now, you lousy....you lousy.....' he said, unable to complete the sentence because of his anger.

'Don't you mean, Now, you lousy Yid?'

That cost me a second blow, this time in my midriff.

'Two men are dead. Murdered. A taxi driver and a guy in Villa apartments. You, Rubin, have been identified. You were there both times.' He paused. 'I think you've some explaining to do, feller.'

Chapter Thirteen

It was Friday afternoon and the faithful had been to prayers.

The roads close by the mosque were crowded with motor cars, parked on the pavements. There were many people, men and boys, moving about on foot.

Finding out where Suleiman Chopdat lived had been easy. He happens to live in a very large house on top of a hill overlooking much of the city.

I took my position outside the front of this house. I didn't have to wait long. A four-door saloon Mercedes Benz, S class, purred down the street. Electronic gates purred open. Everything about Chopdat seemed feline.

The gates did not swing shut immediately and I was able to see inside the Chopdat compound. But I hadn't come here simply to peer inside; I was going to beard Chopdat in his very own den. There were two guards to get past but they were suffering from dereliction of duty. Instead of guarding the entrance, the dozy pair were staring at Chopdat or, perhaps, if truth be known, staring at Choppie's daughters who had emerged from the house to greet the returning men.

I approached the group.

'Mr Chopdat?' I said.

An older man with a religious beard said, 'Which Mr Chopdat do you want?'

That evoked laughter, loud, and far beyond the attempt at humour.

'The one who owns Choppie's Bar,' I said. 'The place where a good Muslim sells alcohol to the masses of this city.'

That went down like......what else?.....a lead balloon.

Chopdat himself spoke. He was clearly the top feeder in the clan.

'Today is difficult, Mr.....'

'Rubin. Jack Rubin.'

'It is difficult, Mr Rubin, because, you will understand, I am a very busy man.' Chopdat said in quiet, measured tones.

'It won't wait,' I said.

'What is it that will not wait?' he asked, smiling thinly.

'It's a delicate matter, Mr Chopdat,' I said. 'Best discussed behind closed doors.'

'I do not know you, Mr....'

'Rubin, I said. 'After what I have to say, you won't have any trouble remembering my name.'

'I think I need more than that, Mr Rubin,' Chopdat said, and he turned his back on me, preparing to go inside.

'Here's another name for you, Choppie,' I said insolently. 'Jessica. Jessica Connelly.'

He stopped, turned.

'Jessica Connelly,' I said again, quieter this time.

'I think you had better come inside, Mr Rubin,' Chopdat said, and he sighed deeply.

I followed Chopdat into the house and along a series of corridors, the house was that big. Girls in saris giggled and flattened themselves against white walls as I passed.

Soon, I was alone in a white room - everything seemed to be about whiteness - alone with Chopdat. On a wall were photographs of Mecca. On a desk, quotations, in Arabic, from the Koran.

'Have you been on the Hajj?' I said.

'Oh yes,' Chopdat said. 'And I am going again next year.'

I knew the reason. He would then be qualified to add *al hajj* to his name.

Mr Rubin, I have many responsibilities.'

That was his way of ordering me to get down to business, the matter that had brought me uninvited to his house.

'I think, Mr Chopdat, that you can assist us with our enquiries,' I said.

'You are not a police officer,' he said.

No hint of a question in his voice. No point in deception.

'My company is Jack Rubin and Associates. I am a private investigator. I have been asked to find a girl. Jessica Connelly.'

'I see.'

'I was asked, I was paid, and paid well, by a Mr Burnside,' I said.

I looked at him closely, expecting a reaction. I detected nothing, apart from the slightest shrug of his shoulders.

'You know Mr Burnside, of course,' I said.

Chopdat shook his head.

'The name is not familiar to me.'

'Bullshit!' I said. 'You know him all right.'

'I can assure you, Mr Rubin -'

'Don't bother lying,' I said, interrupting. 'I saw Burnside go into your office the other evening.'

'Which office is this?'

'Down at Choppie's Bar. Where else?'

'I have many.......establishments,' he replied. 'What date was this?'

I bit my lower lip. I'd jumped in with both feet and the water was proving to be deep. I'd no proof that he had been the one in that office, the one who had left by the back door with Burnside and Frank Conteh. This was not the time to express my doubts. I had to tough it out.

'I was in the bar. I have a witness. Frank Conteh and Mr Burnside both entered your office. And all three of you left by the back door. Are you going to tell me you don't know Frank Conteh?'

My certainty did the trick.

'Frank Conteh I have done business with. Your Mr Burnside....that is not a name I know.'

There was a timid knock on the door. A girl, a young kid, entered with a tray. On the tray were iced drinks and sparkling glasses.

I accepted a glass of lemon water, with a liberal amount of ice. This was a welcome breathing space. I had time to think. Someone was playing silly buggers and it wasn't your truly, Jack Rubin. So either Chopdat was lying through his teeth, or.....or the guy who had come to my office and had paid me four grand was not called Burnside. His cheque had been made out to a company, and the signature was not completely legible. But it had gone through the bank and landed up in my account.

Chopdat drank half of a glass of water. He stood up.

'I think, Mr Rubin, that I must return to my family.'

'Not till you've answered my questions,' I said.

He smiled thinly again.

'You are not a police office,' he said. 'This is my house. I have broken no laws. I am not obliged to answer any questions.'

'I understand what you are saying,' I said.

'Good.'

'I came here to warn you that your life may be in danger.'

Again that smile. 'And what makes you think that, Mr Rubin?'

Two men have died. I was witness to a shooting. A taxi driver.'

'I own a taxi company,' Chopdat said. 'All my employees are accounted for.'

'Yes. But what about the other dead person?'

'The other?'

'I found the decomposing body of a man. It was in a flat he owned, but which he rented out to a woman.'

He did not answer but ostentatiously looked at the watch that he wore on his left wrist.

The dead man was Alfred Coburn and the woman who lives there is.....Jessica.'

'Jessica?' he murmured, for all the world as if this was the first time he had heard that name.

'Jessica Connelly,' I said. And added, looking Chopdat straight in the eye, 'There were photographs.'

Choppie went back to his low couch and sat down again. He drained his glass. I poured more lemon water for myself.

'You say that you are not from the police,' Chopdat said.

'I was a copper for several years but now I'm-'

'A private investigator,' he cut in.

'Let's talk about Frank,' I said.

He sighed. 'I admit to knowing that man. I wish I did not.'

'Why's that, Mr Chopdat?' I asked quietly.

'He is a criminal. A violent person.'

'But you deal with him,' I said.

'A man of a very low class,' he added.

'So why let him into your office?'

'When such a person makes a....a request, it is not easy to deny him.'

'Yes?' I said, barely audible.

He was talking at last and I didn't want to break his train of thought.

'I am a businessman, Mr Rubin. I cannot be responsible for the behaviour of other people. What they do in their private lives......you understand.'

I nodded.

'I do business with Alfred Coburn.'

Put that in the past tense, baby!

'Import and export,' I said.

'Exactly,' Chopdat said. 'Frank Conteh is involved with Mr Coburn.'

'And Mr Burnside?'

'This name, I am not knowing.'

That was the first time that Chopdat had let his use of English slip. He was feeling the pressure.

'So who was the guy accompanied Frank into your office?'

'He was with Frank,' Chopdat said lamely.

'Why would Burnside pay me, and pay me well, to find Jessica?' I said.

'Frank wanted help in finding a woman,' Chopdat said.

'Jessica Connelly.'

'Perhaps.'

'Perhaps? What the hell does that mean?'

'I refused to assist them. I am a businessman. I am not a seeker after lost persons.'

'Are you telling me you don't know this woman?'

'I believe that in the past this woman was a friend of Frank Conteh.'

'Friend? You mean.....girl friend?'

'Perhaps.'

'That word again,' I said.

Chopdat stood up. Moved to the door.

'And now, Mr Rubin. I have work to do.'

'Work? On the Sabbath day?'

Allah didn't rest after the six days of creation and we see no need to rest on our Sabbath which is Friday, the sixth day of the week. The important thing is to meet together for communal prayers.

He smiled at me in his thin and superior way.

'You are a believer, Mr Rubin?'

'I'll tell you what I believe in Choppie,' I said with a fierceness that surprised me. 'I believe in nothing. I think that the human animal is the only animal we need to fear. I don't believe in God or any of that shit. I am an atheist.'

Chopdat stroked his nose. 'I was told you were a Jew,' he said.

Chapter Fourteen

'There's a message from your copper tart,' Malik said. 'She telephoned. I took a message.'

Malik gave me a piece of paper. It was an address.

'So how is it going?' Malik asked.

There was in his voice that peevish edge which indicated he was offended at being excluded.

'I'm now convinced - switch the kettle on, will you? - convinced that Frank killed Alfred Coburn. I don't know why.'

I poured boiling water on to a tea bag. Lemon and ginger. My usual camomile makes me too placid, and this was not the time for that. There was still work to be done.

'Coburn, Choppie and Burnside are involved in something. A money-maker.'

'Drugs,' Malik said.

'Yes. And Big Frank is involved as well.'But there was a falling out. And Frank killed Coburn.'

'So why is Frank looking for the girl? Jessica.'

'I'll know that when I find one or the other,' I said. 'Or both.'

My stomach rumbled. I realised that I was hungry.

'I heard that,' Malik said, grinning.

'Then it's a good job I didn't fart, isn't it?'

We agreed to go out to eat. We went to a new place in an old arcade. The food was good and the prices reasonable.

'Alfred Coburn set Jessica up in her own flat. Paid for everything, rent, council tax, her clothing. Spoiled her rotten in exchange for sex.'

Malik nodded. Stuck his nose into a bowl of pasta and salad.

'Frank was jealous. That's a powerful emotion.'

Again Malik nodded agreement.

We finished the meal. Malik was first to the finishing post. He scoffs, even when he's not hungry.

We walked down Railway Street and across Station Square. At the bottom of the steps to the office, I told Malik to hold the fort.

'You going out again, Mr Rubin.'

'Yes. And don't phone me.'

'What are you looking for this time?' he asked.

'I expect to find the smell of stinking fish,' I said.

'It can't be as bad as that body we found.'

'This is a different kind of stink. And a different kind of fish.' And I added|: 'Keep your cell phone switched on. I might need to ring you.'

Within an hour, after having walked steadily for about three miles, I was outside a large house in the suburbs. Not as large as Chopdat's vulgar palace, but large enough.

There was an iron fence all round the property.

On the gate there was a dial phone. I rang several times and no one answered. Burnside was there all right. I'd had a glimpse of him at a curtained window. And there were two cars in the driveway.

I continued to press the bell. He could hardly ignore me for ever. Finally, a voice came through.

'Go away.'

It was a weary voice.

'Police,' I said, lying, not for the first time that week.

'Your name and rank,' Burnside said.

'Inspector Lestrade.'

'Lestrade?'

It would be just my luck if the little swine had any knowledge of Conan Doyle.

'Drugs squad, I said. 'Open the gate.'

The gate swung open and I strode down the short driveway.

Burnside came to the door. In his right hand, a pistol.

'Mr Rubin! You're not -'

'No, I'm not,' I said.

I could see from his face that James Burnside was a frightened man.

I reached over and took the gun from him. He did not resist. I emptied the magazine and remembered the single shot in the breech. Then I tried to return the gun to him. He refused to take it.

'You....you said you were a police officer.'

'I lied, Mr Burnside. Just as you lied to me.'

I pushed past him and into the house.

'Are you alone here?' I said.

He nodded.

'Is there a Mrs Burnside? Due home from work any minute now.'

He shook his head.

I sat down on a comfortable settee and Burnside followed suit.

'You came to my office with a pack of lies,' I said.

'I paid you good money,' Burnside said.

'Shouldn't that be *drug* money?'

'Now look here, Rubin -'

'*Mr* Rubin,' I said, and don't you forget it.'

By the time I had finished with him he'd be even more of a nervous wreck.

'So tell me, Mr Burnside. Why did you come to my office?'

'Like I said. To find Jessica. We wanted to know where she was.'

'*We*?'

'Alfred Coburn. We were worried for Jessica's safety. I told you all this.'

'When you came to my office, Mr Burnside, Alfred Coburn was dead. The flies were already buzzing about his body.'

Burnside swallowed hard. His pale face became even whiter.

'You know where Alfred is?'

'I found the stinking body, didn't I?' I paused briefly. 'And you killed him, Burnside.'

'No, no!' He was starting to weep. 'It wasn't me.'

'Then tell me who it was,' I said.

'Frank! Frank! Frank....... Conteh.'

I moved a couple of cushions, making myself more comfortable.

I leaned forward earnestly.

'I think I'd better warn you, Mr Burnside. I have spoken at length with your pal Chopdat. He has spilled his guts. Couldn't wait to confess. He told me about the whole drugs operation. And the money laundering.'

'The whole....everything...I'm only an employee. It....it was all Alfred's doing.'

'Very convenient,' I said. 'Put the blame on the one who is dead. Can't give his side of the story.'

'It's the truth. God's truth,' Burnside said.

His words might be lies but there was no doubting the sincerity of his tears, rolling unchecked down his face.

'Why would Frank want to kill Mr Coburn?'

'Because of Jessica,' Burnside said, without hesitation.

'Tell me about her,' I said.

'I love her, Mer Rubin. I have loved her for many years.'

'She's not very old, is she?'

'No,' Burnside said. 'But even before she was sixteen, she was a good-looking kid.'

'While she was under-age. Did you -'

112

'No, no!' Burnside looked shocked. 'Not then, not now.'

'I see. You adored her from afar.'

'Yes.'

'And Mrs Burnside?'

'She left me. About twelve months since,' Burnside said.

'Did you tell your wife that you were....you were enamoured of the lovely Jessica?'

'No, but she guessed.'

I rubbed my chin. I needed a shave.

'So when you came to see me, it was on your own behalf, not Coburn's'

'I was afraid. Still am. Frank is a violent man. He's done time.'

'For what?'

'You name it,' Burnside shrugged.

'No, Mr Burnside, you name it,' I said.

'GBH. Assault with threats. Grand theft auto.'

'A nasty piece of work,' I said.

'Don't tangle with Big Frank,' Burnside warned.

'I intend to do just that,' I said.

'He's hard. He fights dirty. He never knows when he is beaten.'

'Me neither,' I said. 'Me neither.'

Burnside asked me if I'd like something to drink. I declined, and then changed my mind and said I'd drink water. I followed Burnside to the kitchen; didn't want him making a clandestine telephone call, or running out into the garden to his motor car.

'Ice, Mr Rubin?'

'No ice,' I said.

We returned to the sitting room.

I drank the water in one go.

'A last question, Mr Burnside. I heard that Frank changed his name.'

'That's right. In the old days he was always Francis. I think he started using Frank while he was doing time. Francis is hardly a macho name, is it?'

'I'll use your telephone, Mr Burnside,' I said.

It wasn't a request.

I dialled Silcock's number. Getting past the guard dogs was not easy but I made it eventually.

'Jack Rubin here. I'm with a Mr James Burnside.'

I gave the address.

'I think he would like to assist you with your enquiries. And while you're at it, you might like to have a word with Mr Suleiman Chopdat.'

Silcock spat out a couple of expletives and asked me what charges might apply to Chopdat.

'Wife beating, Spitting in the street. Dropping litter. You'll know when Mr Burnside has stopped talking.'

I put down the telephone receiver. Turned to James Burnside.

'I don't think we'll be seeing one another again, Mr Burnside,' I said. 'so if you'd like to make out a cheque.....'

'A cheque? How much?'

'Two thousand bucks should cover it,' I said.

'Two thousand....but I've already given you four grand.'

'Yes, I know.'

'Then what's this for?' Burnside asked.

'Disbursements,' I said. 'We did mention disbursements, Mr Burnside, did we not?'

Chapter Fifteen

So far, everything had been easy. Too easy, you might think. OK, there had been the dead body and the shooting of Charlie Simmonite. For them, I didn't care a toss. Coburn was involved in dirty business deals, and there are few things dirtier than drugs. As for Charlie Simmonite, he was a criminal who drove get-away cars for the likes of Francis 'Big Frank' Conteh. I did not know either of them, and it's impossible to grieve for those you don't know.

Once again I decided to walk. There's something about walking that is better than any other kind of exercise. Not that I was walking in order to improve my health. It was to clear my brain. Get my thoughts into some kind of order.

My only concern was Frank. So everybody said he was a big hard man. Well, there's an old saying. It comes from boxing. The bigger they are, the harder they fall.

And I had an equaliser. The Browning in the side pocket of my lightweight jacket. I was carrying the jacket because it was another warm evening and I'd no wish to arrive in a lather. I'd seen what Frank had done to Coburn using a knife.

Well, a gun was faster and more deadly than a knife. Then I remembered a scene from a movie. *The Magnificent Seven.* This rough cow hand boasts that a gun is always faster than a knife. He draws a reluctant James Coburn into a contest. Coburn has the knife. And in the contest, Coburn is the quicker. It was a good scene, but wasted as far as the rest of the movie is concerned, because there's not a scene where Coburn's prowess with the knife is crucial.

The place where I was now going was the second place which Burnside owned. I suspected that he too, like his pal Coburn, hoped for a little love nest with the lovely girl.

The wise thing would have been to involve Silcock, or even take Malik along with me, but I wanted to be alone with Jessica. Forget Burnside, forget Frank - I wanted this one for myself alone.

The more I walked, the jauntier I felt. Walking causes the muscles to produce the happy hormones, or whatever they are called. I certainly felt happy. I whistled as I walked along.

I should have known better. In all of life there is always the prospect that just when you are feeling confident, you are sure as hell riding for a fall. Pride goes before destruction, and a haughty spirit before a fall.

I reached the house. It was one of those old semi-detached places. There was a small iron gate. I took special care not to allow it to creak as I pushed it open. Someone was at home. There were lights in the lounge, or front room, or whatever they are called. Thick curtains were drawn across the windows but I could just make out the dim flicker of a TV set.

Treading carefully, I went round the back of the house. Here there were no lights. So, still taking care, I went to the front once again. I listened carefully. I tried the door handle, just in case it was unlocked, but it was locked. Sad, but nobody except a bloody domkop fails to lock doors after dark.

I knocked gently on the door. Nobody responded. I knocked again, louder this time. Someone came to the widow and peeked round the curtain. I stood to the left of the door where I could not be seen.

I knocked a third time.

'Who's there?'

A woman's voice.

'Me,' I said, adopting a hoarse voice. 'Let me in.'

A key was turned in the lock.

'Why didn't you bring......'

She had no time to complete the question. I forced myself in and closed the door behind me.

'Good God!' she said, looking in horror at the Browning in my right hand.

A quick search of the two-bedroomed house soon determined that Frank Conteh was not at home. If indeed he had ever lived there.

Back in the lounge, I had time to look at the girl. She was not cowering. I think she'd decided I was not there to kill her. I could see that she was getting all her confidence back.

She was a cracker, I tell you. Not pretty, but beautiful. She was wearing a house robe. Her feet were bare. On her head there was a *doek*. I was familiar with these items from my childhood and early youth in South Africa. A *doek* is a square of cloth worn by women on the head, especially to indicate that they are married. I looked down at the woman's hands: no sign of rings on her fingers.

'So you are the Jessica Connelly I have heard so much about,' I said.

'Who the hell are you?' Jessica asked.

'Jack Rubin,' I said.

'You a cop?'

I shook my head. 'No.'

'Then what's with the water pistol?' she said.

'This is no water pistol, Jessica. This is a deadly weapon.'

'I like men with a deadly weapon,' she said, and she almost smiled.

'And I like girls who like men who carry a deadly weapon.'

'I am not a girl,' she said.

'OK. Young woman. That suit your feminist principles?'

I removed the box magazine and put the gun in my pocket.

'Nice house coat,' I said.

'It's a robe.'

What are you wearing underneath it?' I said.

She gave me a look of withering contempt and flashed open the robe. 'F*** all.'

I averted my eyes, but not till I'd clocked all I needed to see.

'Don't us that kind of language with me, Jessica.'

'What did you say your name was?'

Jack. Jack Rubin.'

'Do you ever swear, Jack Rubin?'

'All the time,' I said. 'But I'm a man.'

'And that makes it OK for you but not for me,' Jessica sneered.

'Yes, it does! I'm not a puritan, but women cussing....I don't like it.'

'Who the hell are you, mister,' Jessica said assertively.

'I told you -'

.Sure, your name. But who are you? What you lookin' for, man? What do you want?'

'Right now, Jessica, I want you,' I said.

I smiled a full flashing smile. the one that's supposed to break women's hearts, or at least weaken their resolve. Believe me, it works, most of the time.

'Do you always carry a gun when you're feeling randy?'

Her lips were thin. Her eyebrows had been shaved off and then pencilled in again. Her skin was very pale, the skin of her face, and made paler by a liberal application of powder.

'What are you staring at?' Jessica asked.

'You, baby.'

'I'm no baby, Rubin. Or can't you see that?'

Burnside had said he'd kill for her. Frank already had. How many others were in the line?

'Where's Frank?' I said.

'Go to hell,' Jessica said.

Her voice was harsher than her photographs had suggested.

'He's a killer, Jessica, and very dangerous.'

'What's that to me, eh? What's that to me?'

I wanted to slap her face. Slap some sense into her, not punishment.

'You're a beautiful girl,' I said. 'Why do you keep the company of criminals?'

'Such as?'

Alfred Coburn. James Burnside. Frank Conteh.'

'Do I tell you ....do I choose your friends?' she snapped.

'You don't even know me,' I said.

'No, Mr Clever-Dick Rubin, and you don't know me.' She paused. 'So why don't you get lost before I call the police?'

Two steps and I slapped her hard across the face. She staggered but she did not fall. Nor did she weep. This was one tough *vrou*.

I removed her hand from her face and gently stroked her myself. Then I took hold of her shoulders and kissed her on the mouth. At first she seemed resistant and then she relaxed into my arms.

Soon we were on the settee and kissing deeply, exploring with our tongues. My fingers moved gently to open her robe.

'No, Jack,' she said, drawing the robe tightly about her body. 'Not now.'

'Later, Jessica,' I said. 'I must have you.'

And as soon as I'd spoken the words, I knew I was a silly doos. Had I forgotten my own rule? Treat 'em mean, keep 'em keen.

Jessica stood up.

'Would you like something to drink, Jack?' she asked.

I shook my head.

'I believe you enjoy dancing,' I said.

'How do you know that?'

'Something a little bird told me,' I said, laughing. 'So how about we go out dancing?'

'Are you mad?' she said. 'You come in here, gun in hand, you slap me around. And now you suggest going out for the evening.'

'Yes or no, Jessica?'

'Yes,' she said.

And treated me to a magnificent smile, all teeth and sincerity.

'Get your glad rags on and then we can go.'

'Do you have wheels?' Jessica said.

'We can call a taxi.'

She told me there were beers in the fridge. I wasn't interested.

I followed her into the bedroom.

Chapter Sixteen

The room smelled of Jessica. It was a good smell.

There are beers in the fridge,' she said.

I smiled.

'Are you trying to get me out of your bedroom?' I said.

'I can't get ready to go out if you are going to stand there, staring at me.'

She could see me through he dressing room mirror.

'We don't have to go out,' I said.

'It was your idea,' Jessica answered.

Her bed looked inviting. All it needed was for me to take off her robe, and human desire would do the rest.

There was a telephone on the small bedside cupboard. It was modern and girlish, in pink. I wondered who had bought Jessica that expensive toy, Alfred Coburn or James Burnside.

'Get a beer. Watch the TV,' Jessica said.

I shrugged my agreement. At the same time I checked the windows. I reached over and removed a key from the window lock.

'What's the matter?' Jessica asked.

'Hm?'

'Do you think I'm going to climb out of the window?

'Not now, you're not, darling,' I said, waving the small key under her pert nose.

It really was a lovely nose. I reached out and touched her hair and kissed her head gently. The start of the famous Jack Rubin seduction technique.

She did not respond. I took hold of her shoulders. Still no response. And, I noticed, she did not smile. In fact, she had not smiled once since I had broken into her home, waving the Browning about.

I did not let go of her shoulders.

'You're a very beautiful woman, Jessica,' I said.

This was not my usual tactic. Treat 'em mean and keep 'em keen has always worked for me. I don't mean that I followed Nietzsche's advice to carry a whip when going top a woman but I have learned that it pays best not to be too effusive. Now I was like an acne'd swain, complimentary, daft as a brush.

'I could see how beautiful you were from the moment I fist saw your photo,' I said.

She spun round.

'What do you mean? Saw my photo?'

There was anger in her brown eyes.

'James Burnside had a photograph. He showed me. And then were were more in Alfred Coburn's wallet. Alfred Coburn. There were photographs in his wallet,' I said.

'You saw him?'

'I saw him dead. In the apartment he keeps for you.'

'Dead? How did -'

'Stabbed,' I said.

'What did he look like?'

'He didn't have rosy cheeks,' I said. 'He looked very dead. Another twenty-four hours and he'd have been able to get to the morgue without any assistance.'

'As bad as that?' she said quietly.

'Worse, much worse,' I said.

'Who......who did it, Jack?'

She was soft again, leaning in to me.

'That's what I'm trying to find out,' I said. 'I'm a private investigator. James Burnside paid me-'

'Oh, him! He's a complete domkop.'

She again turned to look in the mirror.

'He's crazy about you, Jessica. He paid me good money to find you.'

'Are you Burnside's friend?' she said.

I shook my head. Told her how Burnside had turned up out of the blue, rushed into my office, money no object, find this girl.

'Please, Jack. Go into the other room. Get a beer.'

'Watch TV,' I said, sneering.

'Play music,' she said.

I did as she suggested. I took a beer from the refrigerator. Drank from the bottle.

There was a CD player. I checked the stack of discs. Most of it was not my kind of music. I found a Tom Jones compilation.

Tom was belting out the *Green, Green Grass of Home* when Jessica came out of the bedroom. Well, not quite out. She leaned seductively at the door.

'I like that,' Jessica said. 'Turn the volume up, Jack.'

It seemed too loud already but Jessica was in the other room and the door was closed, so what the hell.

I drank my beer. I felt at ease with myself and the world.. I was taking a beautiful girl out for the evening, as beautiful a piece as I'd ever seen in my life. We'd get to dance and dine, and afterwards, back at her place I would have what I most desired. I was confident that I could be as good with Jessica as I had been with many girls before her.

Finally, the bedroom door opened. Tom Jones was singing a golden oldie about a tart who had deceived him. Delilah was the name. As soon as I saws Jessica, I switched off the music. Jessica Connelly in a house coat, carpet slippers and a *doek* on her head had been some looker. Now, though, she was wearing a black evening gown, her face made up, a shining wig on her head, high-heeled shoes. Twenty minutes earlier I'd have said such a transformation was not possible. Now I was ready to believe that there are angels with wings flying about in the sky, giving attendance to this vision of loveliness.

'It was worth the wait, Jessica,' I said quietly, not wishing to break the spell.

'Did you phone for a taxi?' she asked.

I shook my head, felt foolish. 'I'm a twat, a *doos*,' I said.

I laughed but had no response from Jessica.

I used my cell phone to call a taxi. They were busy and I should expect a car to arrive after thirty minutes.

I sat down on the settee and took Jessica in my arms. I kissed her.

'Don't spoil my hair,' she said.

So damn romantic! I smiled. She did not not return my smile. I began to wonder if she had teeth. But I knew she had, for my tongue had explored while we kissed.

I was hungry for her but I'd have to wait.

There was a knock at the door.

'OK!' Jessica called.

The taxi driver had arrived early.

Now Jessica took the initiative. She reached over, took hold of my hair and pulled me in close to her body. Her kiss was passionate. Like me, she was on heat. Or so I thought.

But I saw, briefly, that she was looking not at me, but over my shoulder.

Then, suddenly, there was a movement of the air behind me. I half turned. I saw the knife. It came down in an arc, swiftly, and cut across my shoulder. I felt intense pain.

Jessica pushed me and I dropped to the floor. I was on one knee. The blade had cut into my left shoulder. Lucky for me, I am right-handed.

The guy came at me, determined to cut me again, and this time in a deadly place.

Despite the pain, I managed to roll over and get out of reach of the knife blade. I felt in my pocket for the Browning.

The other guy moved quickly. He kicked the gun from my hand. It landed just beyond my reach.

He took his eyes off me and dived to get the gun. I stuck out my leg and the guy fell heavily.

I also went to for the gun. The pain in my shoulder was intense but survival was my priority. As my fingers reached for the Browning, the other guy got a grip on my throat. He had a powerful grip, large hands.

In the usual way I'd have been a match for him but I was losing blood fast and that weakened me. As his fingers tightened on my throat, I could tell I was beginning to lose consciousness.

I had been tricked, played for a sucker. By Jessica, the beautiful girl. She had played me like an angler plays a fish. As, no doubt, she had played Alfred Coburn and James Burnside, and who knows how many other foolish men. Instead of thinking straight, using my brain, I'd been thinking with my dick, and that's not thinking at all.

And the upshot was that I was bleeding badly and being strangled by Big Frank Conteh.

My body went limp. I did not struggle. Did not try to wrench his hands from my throat.

Frank removed his fingers from my windpipe. He laughed out loud. He relaxed and made to stand up. His head was sideways on to me. I summoned up all the strength that remained to me and hit him hard on the temporal region at the side of his head.

His hands went to the site of the pain. I gained my feet and kicked him hard on the shin. Down there the fibula bone is thin and Frank felt the pain. He started to fall. This was my chance. I kicked him hard in the face. Blood spurted from his nose. That was two of us bleeding and in pain.

Frank Conteh was far from finished. He grunted and roared with pain. He sprung forward, a kind of rugby tackle, and took me by the ankles. I crashed to the floor, my left shoulder hitting first. But I was now beyond pain.

At such moments we have no idea of the passing of time. I did not even see Jessica Connelly, save as a distant and peripheral figure, somewhere in that room. My complete attention was on Frank, and on survival. That he meant to kill me, I did not doubt.

Death by strangulation has never held any appeal to me. Death by any means, for that matter.

We fought, kicked, punched, scratched even. Frank spat hard in my face. One minute we were on the floor and the next hitting the wall. The room was a complete shambles.

My strength was ebbing fast. But so was Frank's.

At one stage, I was kneeling on the floor, fighting for breath. Frank was over the other side. He was getting to his feet again. Many another man would long since have gone down and stayed down but Frank was a big, tough guy.

Near to me was a small wooden stool. It seemed to be made of black wood, ebony perhaps. A hard wood. I grabbed the stool and threw it with what remained of my strength. It was about to strike Frank on hos body but just then he slipped and he took the full force of the stool on his face. He had not looked pretty before, but now, with more blood pouring from his nose and other wounds, he looked like something from a horror comic, bloodied and dangerous.

Frank screamed with rage and pain. He spotted the knife, grabbed it in his right hand, and lunged at me.

I tried to get to my feet. I was too slow. And too weak to defend myself. This was the moment of truth. I was going to die from multiple stab wounds.

'NO!!!!!'

Jessica's commanding voice filled the room.

'Francis!!! NO!!'

Frank Conteh stopped. The knife in his upraised hand. Blood and savagery on his face.

Jessica stood between us. In her hand, my Browning.

I summoned up the last of my strength and courage and got to my feet.

'Move!' Frank roared.

'No, Francis! Enough is enough.'

'Move out of the way,gel,' Frank shouted.

It all happened faster than words can tell. One moment Jessica was pleading with Frank to stop and the next he was moving toward her with the knife in his hand.

Then came the crack of the pistol. Frank seemed to stop in his tracks. Then he fell, and the knife with him. Jessica had fired into his chest. On the man's face there was a stare of utter disbelief. He fell heavily to the floor, blood spurting from his chest, as if a large artery had been severed.

'Jessica....' I said.

She turned to me, full face. In her eyes there was wildness.

'You....you pig,' she screamed, and pulled the trigger.

There was a click.

Jessica looked at me, expecting me to fall wounded.

I moved over to her and took the Browning out of her hand.

'There was only one bullet,' I said. 'The one in the breech.'

I put the gun in my pocket, along with the box of cartridges.

Jessica fell on her knees beside Frank Conteh. She was weeping and wailing.

I placed an arm round her shoulder - my right arm, not the useless left one.

'I....I'm sorry, Jessica,' I said.

'Sorry my arse,' she snarled, and at that moment no longer looked beautiful.

Tears falling from her eyes were spoiling the powder on her face. He shining black wig had fallen off. It was as if she were a different person, a different race.

'I understand, Jessica,' I said, anxious to give her a measure of comfort.

'You understand, Jack Shit!' Jessica said, getting control of her crying.

'I know that Frank was your husband and that your name is Jessica Conteh,' I said.

She looked hard at me, no tears now. On her face, a look of utter contempt.

'You rotten men!' she spat. 'You're as stupid as all the others. Why are men so....so stupid?'

'If he wasn't your husband,' I said, 'then who the hell was he?'

'Francis. He wasn't my husband. He.......he is my brother.'

Chapter Seventeen

Chief Superintendent Silcock looked very serious.

'Two deaths on my patch in just one week,' he said. 'I don't like it, Jack.'

'Did I kill them?'

'You seem to attract trouble,' he said.

I'd have shrugged my shoulders, if it had not been for the pain and the stitches, and the fact that it isn't all that easy to shrug when you're lying in bed in a hospital unit. A private hospital too, but I could afford it.

'So who killed Coburn?' Silcock asked.

'No idea,' I said.

'Could it have been the girl?'

'I doubt it,' I said. 'She doesn't seem the type.'

Failing to mention that she'd pulled the trigger on me, after despatching of her own brother. I've always been a sucker where pretty girls are concerned.

'We'll find her,' Silcock said.

I did not quarrel with him. But I knew that Jessica could pass for black as well as white.

'Coburn and Burnside were involved in some kind of dirty work,' I said.

'There shouldn't be too much trouble breaking Burnside down,' Silcock said.

'And you might want to talk to Choppie.'

'He's smart,' Silcock said. 'Knows how to cover his tracks.'

A young nurse entered.

'This man giving you trouble?' Silcock asked her. 'If he does, ring the police, and ask for me.'

The girl checked my temperature, pulse and respiration rates.

My second visitor, arriving shortly after Silcock left, was Sergeant Brigid Riley. She brought me fruit, biscuits, chocolate.

'I'm being discharged tomorrow,' I said.

'So soon?'

'They charge by the hour,' I said.

'Ill come round to your place,' she said. 'I'm on the morning shift this week.'

"Wait until my shoulder has mended,' I said.

'What I had in mind did not involve using your shoulder,' she said, smiling. 'Where is the woman, Jessica, now,' Brigid asked, sounding every inch the copper.

I told her that I did not know but I guessed she had legged it to some place far away.

My third visitor was Malik, accompanied by Mona, his wife. They had also come armed with food.

Next day, Malik came to the clinic in his Merc. He was my lift home. It was good to be back in my own house, away from the concrete and girders of the city, with a view of the treeless uplands.

'It's good to be alive, Malik,' I said.

The kitchen heaved with food.

Malik switched on the kettle.

"What do you want? Camomile or green tea?' he asked.

'Have you forgotten the rule? So soon? We make our own tea.'

'And we never discuss religion.' Malik said.

'Especially that,' I said.

I had a sling on my left shoulder.

'I think I'll go mad and have lemon and ginger,' I said, reaching up for a tea bag.

I felt pain. Soon be time to take my pain killers again.

We drank tea. Malik told me the amount in our bank account. It was a healthy sum. Jack Rubin Associates was proving to be a viable business.

'This Jessica tart,' Malik said.

'Yes?'

'Did you.....did you -'

I shook my head.

'She's the one who got away,' I said.

'Did she kill Coburn?' Malik asked, and turned up his nose as if he too remembered the stink of that dead body.

'Probably,' I said, and I sighed. 'It goes to show.'

'Show what?' Malik asked.

'When lovely woman stoops to folly,

And finds too late that men betray,

What charm can soothe her melancholy,

'What art can wash her guilt away?'

Malik smiled with confidence. He'd become accustomed to my quotations. The detritus of a decent education.

'Shakespeare!'

'No,' I said, 'not Shakespeare.'

'Explain one thing to me, Mr Rubin.' Malik said.

'Shoot!' I said, and realised it didn't sound too appropriate, after what I'd just been under.

'Maybe I'm stupid,' Malik said.

'I wouldn't argue with that,' I said, smiling.

'If Frank Conteh and Jessica were, as you say, brother and sister....but they couldn't be,' he concluded.

'Why couldn't they be?'

'Well, because he is black and she is white.'

Strange, how we refer to the recently dead in the present tense. But this was no time to discuss this, and Malik was not the person to discuss it with. He's happier with account sheets, profit and loss accounts, putting money into the business account.

'I think they must have been half-brother and half sister. I've seen it in South Africa. some children are quite dark and some can pass for white.'

'But she didn't need to hide the fact she was a Coloured,' Malik said, and immediately corrected himself to 'mixed race.'

'Who knows what drives people to do what they do?' I said rhetorically.

Within a week, the sling was off and the stitches had dissolved.

I drove into the city and parked at Central.

The young woman on Reception, a civilian, smiled at me. I was a better proposition than the drunks, chavs and lunatics she saw on a regular basis.

Within five minutes I was in Silcock's office. I told him as much as I thought he needed to know and again omitted my suspicions about who it was killed Alfred Coburn. About who killed Charlie Simmonite, there was no doubt - that was Big Frank.

Silcock checked his watch. 'I have a meeting,' he said.

'Can I have a quick word with David Lunn?' I said.

Silcock shouted and Lunn came in from an adjacent office. He stared at me with deep and bitter loathing. This was a guy I'd never harmed in my life. Just beaten him at exams and other tests while we were undergoing initial training, that's all. And, of course, he had this idea I was Jewish, and I haven't seen the inside of a synagogue since my *bar mitzvah*.

I walked over to Lunn, smiling broadly. He did not return my smile.

I was still smiling when I drew back my right fist and punched him hard in the solar plexus.

He went down and stayed down.

Silcock looked serious, but there was laughter in his eyes as he pointed to the door.

I took the hint, massaging my knuckles as I went.